SHARDS

A Dark Mystery

by

Tom Piccirilli

A Write Way Publishing Book

Write Way Publishing
10555 E. Dartmouth, Ste 210
Aurora, CO 80014

First Edition; 1996

ISBN 1-885173-23-7

1 2 3 4 5 6 7 8 9

For Bill Piccirilli
because brothers take another beating
in this one

I'd like to acknowledge the following people for their encouragement, assistance, suggestions and friendship: Sue Storm, Jack Cady, Ed McFadden, Adam Meyer, Kevin Lindenmuth, Lawrence Greenberg, and Lee Seymour, who all lent a hand at just the right time; Ed Gorman, Bill Pronzini, Peter Straub and Lawrence Block, who teach through the finest example; Gerard "I can turn every offbeat comment into a story" Houarner and Linda "It's a boot strap" Addison; Barbara Malenky, who vexes this Yankee; extra special thanks to Jim D'Angelo, Jim Sprague, Glen Coyle, Andy Macejko, Jim Derasmo, and Darryl "I still haven't graduated college, but don't give a damn anymore" Reece, for all the years and beers; the wraiths of Jim Thompson, Cornell Woolrich and James M. Cain, with respect and gratitude. You all own a piece of this. Try not to cut yourselves.

To J.B. and M.O.B. because they sent me out there in the first place.

And to S.K.H., who still holds the sharpest sliver.

1

"I would never hurt you," he said, taking me in his hand, and
hurting me. The rage coiled around my neck, soft and warm, whispering in my ear like every sin I'd ever passed on, now returning
to seduce me.

I had just split with Linda and was cruising out to Montauk
Point. The night, and its bitter autumn cold, didn't keep the
loneliness and temper in check. The two-hour drive to the
Point wouldn't do any good, but I'd get away from everyone
else for a while. It was necessary. Nobody wants to be around
a broken-hearted writer, especially when he's been reading up
on the fifteen most efficient ways to kill.

So I was taking my frustrations to Montauk, where I could
stare out at the lighthouse and into the waves. It felt good to
be at the tip of Long Island, facing thirty-five hundred miles
across the Atlantic at Portugal, alone in darkness except for
the wind and whispers. Even during the dog days of summer
you could catch a chill lying across those icy boulders. The
rocks were comforting against my fear and depression, and I
could relate to them in a way I no longer could with my girl.

It was October. An atmosphere of ugly intent and purpose had picked up steam halfway through the month and hopefully wouldn't last past Halloween. The dead leaves on the road blew wildly over my hood as I passed the sign for Westhampton, the bed and breakfast town where Linda and I had first made love. We had taken her son Randy up the North fork to a Pumpkin Patch/Petting Zoo in Southhold; he'd enjoyed feeding the animals, riding the pony, braving goblins and witches who'd set up in the haunted tent. I think I liked the place even more than he did, though. Randy was three years old, and I wondered when he would start trying to grab hold of all that was around him before sitting alone and shouting at Portugal.

It had been a wonderful day at the zoo. There was a llama named Frankie who grew infatuated with me from the moment I walked by and fed him a handful of sugar cone. For the rest of the day he followed me around the zoo, trying to neck. Linda laughed and called me "Llama Lips," moving as if to kiss me and then rushing off, swinging Randy in her arms, both of them giggling, "No, Llama Lips! No!"

Life with Frankie the Llama couldn't be much worse than what Linda and I wound up putting each other through. I didn't know how or when it had turned. My thoughts weaved on the black road like silhouettes of children running in front of the car. Sunrise Highway headed into night. In three AM darkness the rest of the world played smart, staying in bed and curled beneath covers with another warm body. The busted fan of my heater droned on. The numbing repetition of noise helped relieve the ache when a thing in its death throes still got three or four good kicks into my chest.

Twigs were swept beneath my tires. I stamped on the accelerator and brought it up to ninety-five. The beer rattling in the cooler on the backseat reminded me of other jaunts I'd taken after other failed relationships; I'd started new books while sitting on the cold rock at the base of the lighthouse. By the time the sun rose I'd be drunk and have a notebook filled with fragments of ideas and stanzas of awful poetry. It would work.

So maybe I was dead, maybe only wounded; there comes a time when you can't tell, when, for the moment, you don't want to know the difference.

My engine screeched and I topped off at a hundred and five, the valve job holding, rods creaking. I was waiting for someone, for anything: it would come; the crash of divine choir, an angel with a flaming sword, maybe a high colonic, or just hitting an oil slick.

Occasionally, a stabbing pain prodded me above the navel; I fought to keep from grunting and tucking up my knees. I dropped to seventy-five and spun gravel when the highway petered out to a winding road. Irate taxpayers had strung up a sign on a bridge, telling all of us to **LEAVE NEW YORK BEFORE IT'S TOO LATE**. Smashed pumpkins littered the underpass.

The heater continued to whine. I drove down the road to Montauk Park, recalling when my father and I played whiffle ball and ate hot dogs with too much chili on the day the police dug up our backyard and my brother D.B. was killed. My father would always be a vision of slickness, as well as madness, rather than one of cancer-ridden weakness and pity. I didn't regret the fact he'd called the police and set D.B. up in a trap. I was only sorry his plan to throw suspicion from himself worked relatively well, and my brother took the fall for the murders alone.

He hadn't escaped unscathed. The reporters and detectives followed us for years, but couldn't tally enough evidence. True crime books followed by the dozen. I read them all. The best was entitled *The Master of Hounds*. D.B. had started on dogs before working his way to children.

Living less than a mile from the cemetery where my father is buried—even if I'm only going out for a morning jog or to take in a movie and a slice of pizza—I tend to wind up cutting through the graveyard. I talked a lot. I talked too much, and still cared too much for answers I never got.

Sitting there on the tombstone and speaking to him aloud was different from recollecting the hours I spent seated beside his deathbed, trying hard not to laugh. The graveyard made for good inspiration every once in a while: since I'm a *Jr.*, it often got me reflecting on my own death, staring at my name on the headstone that way. **NATHANIEL FOLLOWS**. It even sounded as if he wanted me to walk his path, urging me behind him. It helped in plotting murder, solving crimes, and creating and catching psychopathic killers in my books.

I'd injected my fictional Private Eye Jacob Browning with a worldliness I didn't have myself. It made for an odd conflict between us, with him having the edge in experience, sophistication, sordidness, and animal magnetism. In turn, I killed him off—I'd brought him back from the dead two times in three books, but most readers didn't seem to mind the game. If Arthur Conan Doyle could resurrect Sherlock Holmes, and Ian Fleming could resuscitate James Bond, then every now and then I could let Jacob Browning fall out of a ten-story window and land on a life-saving shrub.

Flowing, rolling, the rage went *uh huh uh huh uh huh, c'mon*, licking at my ear.

I parked my car in a hideaway spot towards the border of a thicket and grabbed the cooler, a battery-powered lantern, my notebook, and a couple blankets from the back. The lighthouse wasn't much really, and hadn't worked for years; George Washington had ordered it built, and over the last two-and-a-half centuries the shoreline had become so eroded the lighthouse was in jeopardy of falling into the ocean.

I settled on the rocks, turned the lantern on and started drinking, watching the ocean in the moonlight and listening to waves swish. I rolled old conversations around in my head, still hanging on to the bitterness, it hanging me; throwing myself into the work was a defense mechanism that broke down as much as it ran.

The shrieking didn't last long; I was tired. Words swirled. I finished my fifth beer in one pull. The notebook unfolded to an empty page. I would get P.I. Jacob Browning into a few suspenseful scrapes, and he would lay all the women I wanted to lay and stand for something I knew didn't exist. His muscles would be corded, his beard stubble sexy, and he'd be able to drink a bottle of bourbon without tossing his guts. Browning would walk the streets and call men like myself wimps or gimps, and I would let him get kicked in the balls and shot a few times for it.

Waves lapped at me like Linda. Wind tousled my hair into my eyes as I jotted preliminary notes, circling sentences in the shape of Linda's lips. The perpetual frown on my face was now a scowl, and for the last few hours I'd become increasingly aware of the number of wrinkles in my forehead.

The lighthouse whistled, its rotted upper beams dappled with disintegrating birds' nests. I did my best not to let my thoughts twist in the darkness, though nothing else would stay with me except Linda's mouth. The sea had a way of both attracting and distracting my attention at the same time. Tendrils of mist crept across my legs, flicking at my chest; the rage hissed at the fog. I groaned and drank another beer, and choked on it halfway down.

It took another hour of staring at the froth before I started writing, the sentences coming, but incredibly ugly. My script looked cruel and unnatural, like an EEG graph. *Uh huh, c'mon.* I had a skeletal outline to work with, and I'd come up with a couple of tangled murders that Browning would have to unsnarl. By chapter three he'd already gotten laid and had his ribs broken. That wasn't a bad trade. I offered up an appeal and dug into the story for the next twenty minutes, my handwriting slowly becoming more human.

I stood, stretched, and tossed a couple rocks into the black ocean. Something wanted to make me smile but I couldn't quite let it. I thought about drowning. Several ideas shot past and I let them go because there were enough murders in my head to pack the new novel.

The breeze skimmed past and caught the pages of my notebook, flipping them faster and faster as I watched, until it flew off on the wind, skittering across the rocks. I made a grab for it and missed. I scrambled up a ridge of boulders, and clutched the book before it got away.

As I turned back I noticed that, over on the sand, perhaps a hundred yards away, a small campfire flickered. I stepped back, ashamed, suddenly angry again, and, ridiculously, feeling violated.

A young woman sat like another piece of rock, cut from shadow, carved from night, hugging her knees and staring into the flames. The ridge had blocked my vision of her.

I hesitated, unsure of the next move, if I should make it, if there should be one at all. She obviously craved solitude as much as I did. Staring up at the lighthouse, I thought, *I really don't want to be alone.* Isolation is more than enclosure, it's suffocating. The healing process is slow and fickle.

I didn't want to spook her, and any guy sitting out on the Point at four-thirty on a freezing morning had to be at least a tad crazy. But then again, she was out here.

Maybe I should have been scared. I bit the inside of my cheek waiting for blood, but none came. My curiosity was already raised beyond any writer's endurance, so I went to the cooler, grabbed another bottle, and cleared my throat loudly from a distance in the hope she wouldn't think I was sneaking up on her. When I saw she was looking at me I walked over, proffered the beer, and said, "Hello."

"Hi," she said, taking the bottle with a soft giggle. "I saw you over there when I first got here, but you looked involved with something and I didn't want to disturb you." Good, she'd missed the shrieking. "But I guess I knew that sooner or later we would have to talk. You can't share an entire beach with someone and not even get around to introducing yourself." She had a loud high-pitched titter that didn't chafe my nerves.

She took a couple of large gulps, letting the beer sit in her mouth before swallowing. "There's something solemn about the Point at the end of the night. It's desolate but beautiful, and the lighthouse always looks as though it wants to be a part of the action."

I didn't agree, but said, "I know exactly what you mean."

Flames threw thriving shadows over her face, and she shivered as a chill went through her. Watching her, I felt it, too.

"It's like you can simply reach your arm out and touch France."

"Portugal," I said, nodding as I described her in my mind, already translating my initial reaction into words, wondering if she would be a suitable heroine in some story, or an adequate victim.

Twenty years old on the outside, and probably closer to eighteen, she was dressed in a huge sweater that wasn't so loose you didn't notice she had a nice, compact shape. Jacob Browning might have described her as "a tomato" and would've been screwing her before the blue returned to the sky.

I thought she was incredibly cute, which is more personable and less intimidating than beautiful. I held no such notions of making love to her within the next hour and a half, but the rage pressed my groin.

At first, she looked like Linda; all women were in direct competition with her. Every face started as hers and lingered there before taking on its own reality. The girl's lips were full and luscious, but not as sensuous as Linda's; her eyes glistened with mischief and intellect, but were not so deep. Most importantly, I didn't hate her.

"So what's it all about?" she asked, cutting through the introductory small talk. "You being here looking so stoic? I've never seen anyone glare like you do."

"I don't know," I answered.

"That's not true."

It was. "It is."

"I suspect a broken heart."

"Okay," I said.

"Her fault or yours?"

I sat across the fire from her. "A little of both, but maybe that's just wishful thinking. The accents were on her need for independence and my emotional insecurities." Also, after what my father and brother had taught me, I was much too afraid for her son.

"Now isn't that a switch!" She laughed, and I was surprised the corners of my mouth lifted, too; it felt as if someone was manually pressing my face. "Did your friends bust your chops over that or did you tell them she wanted to settle down but you just don't go in for that shit?"

Her cynical tinge seemed faked, but I'd been wrong about that kind of thing before. "Sounds like you've had a few troubles with the opposite sex yourself."

She gestured obscurely. "Maybe." She drank some beer and asked, "What were you scribbling down over there? Or is that question already an invasion of privacy?"

I shrugged. I never like admitting I'm a novelist because people invariably have not read my books and never plan to. I wouldn't mind that fact if only it wasn't thrown in my face so often. But she had the kind of eyes that always seemed to be pleading, and there was no way I could come up with a quip fast enough while staring into them. "I'm a novelist."

"Really? What's your name?"

"Llama Lips."

Waves roared beside us. They sounded, and even smelled, like torrid animals. The girl had one of those smiles that was actually a self-conscious grin—similar to my own. "Oh yeah," she said. "Wait a second. Didn't you write *Of Llamas and Men?*"

"Yeah, as well as *Lady Chatterly's Llama.*"

The fire started to die. We walked the nearby dunes and gathered as much driftwood and tree branches as we could. My stomach coiled. Pain sliced again, and I almost fell on my face. I returned and gathered the cooler, lantern, and blankets, and brought them to her campfire.

We sat under the blankets, and I found myself talking at ease. I told her how the cracks in my ceiling looked like Lucille Ball's profile; my mother's terrible waffles; the broken paper-feed on my printer, my autographed copy of *Howl* signed by Allen Ginsberg at the Walt Whitman House; the books I'd studied about efficient killing; and how bad I felt to have just had one of my dogs put to sleep. Homer was fourteen and had gone as blind as his namesake, and now every day I saw how Ulysses and Achilles sniffed and probed under the couch, searching for him. I didn't talk about Linda. Somewhere in there I told her my name and she told me hers was Susan Hartford.

It got weird because she started crying, and by then I was drunk enough to do the same, if I'd been able. Intense memories lost their sharpness, blurred, and became blunt. The blood taste in my mouth thickened. I held her and she wept against my chest, not bothering to tell me why. There were no soothing words to say, so I said nothing. The popping sparks and churning sea were satisfactory for the time being.

Like the waves, she had a certain rough and tumble manner, a coming and going presence about her. Several times she began to say something only to clamp her jaws shut and stifle a groan. She was better at it than me; I moaned a little.

"You don't understand," she finally said.

I almost laughed. "No, I don't."

"Things are bad."

"That I do understand."

"Really bad."

"Worse than my Mom's waffles?"

"Yes," she said.

"Uh-oh."

"You wouldn't understand," she repeated.

I said, "Okay."

Seconds ticked off slower than before. Susan looked at me in a way that made me lose my breath. She chuckled sadly, the sound of someone who's become so numb and jaded she can swallow shards of glass without effort. Her hand came up to touch my cheek, but she stopped before her fingers reached me, frozen in mid-air, as if she'd hit a wall.

That single gesture, like other motions, carried a greater significance. I was never more certain of anything in my life. I didn't know what the significance was, or what it would entail or mean to me in the end, but the power behind it was enough to sober me.

She stopped crying, and her eyes lost their pleading edge and were suddenly tough and worn—old, cracked, and beaten. Mine were worse, I thought, but maybe not. I lifted my hand to complete the circuit. As I came up to interlace fingers she dropped her fist to her lap and said, "It would make no sense to you."

"Give it a try. Nonsense and I are old friends."

I could see the instant was already gone, fading into the controlled cold behind her stare. I wished I had that particular gift. She wasn't going to tell me anything, and I was in no position to pressure her. I'd wait and something would happen; I had nothing better to do, and neither did she.

In each other's laps, we split the last beer. She started to fall asleep, snapping awake with the same jumpy starts I get when nightmares and memories merge, and the voices are almost in the room. I eased her down against my chest and laid back in the sand.

"It's okay, Susan."

"Death is everywhere," she murmured. I nodded. A lengthening pause. I groaned again. Sleepily, she asked, "Would you like to make love to me now?"

"Yes."

She moved beneath the blanket easily enough and took off her panties, carefully folded them, and put them behind our heads. I shivered. My hands were freezing, but she led them between her legs; she gasped as I stroked her inner thigh. Linda and I had ended this same way hours ago, just before the fight, her gaze on the ceiling. My knees tightened, and I fought dry heaves, caught up in two women, in the rage, in unfinished lust now about to finish with the wrong lady.

There are times you are too much of yourself, when you are aware you are alive under your skin. My groin stirred, but not enough. The beer roared, rushed my skull, and there was something biting now. Susan undid my pants and reached in to cup my balls, bouncing them playfully and stroking my semi-hard shaft. She had a loving grace. Perhaps that's what stopped me, the hint of love. I looked into the fire and then out at sea. She undid her blouse halfway, exposing her breasts, waiting for me to suck. I did, more a child than a lover. She stared at me, massaged my balls again, waiting for me to do my part. I swallowed. She buttoned her blouse, took my hand in hers and kissed my fingers, then my mouth.

"No?" She wasn't angry, just perplexed.

"No," I said. It was almost a question, too.

She was kind enough to give me an escape route, nuzzling my throat. "Stoic and burning. You're in that whole 'recently had my feelings trampled upon' plight, where you have to go through a mourning period, and hate all members of the opposite sex for at least forty-eight hours."

"No."

She yawned and cuddled closer, hand under my shirt, stroking my chest. "Shit, it was that recent, huh? Yep. Snuggling's fun, but anything more is going to take an awful lot of energy we just don't have at the moment. Don't be worried."

I wasn't, and couldn't figure out why.

"Do you want to smoke some grass?" she asked.

"No."

"It might help."

"It would make it worse, believe it or not."

Again her mouth worked, but she said nothing. Eyebrows arching, she scanned the horizon, searching for the sun. We were a half hour away from dawn, with the black weight of the east lightening the slightest amount, turning the softest shade of blue.

Susan shifted in my arms; the breeze brushed my ears and I scrunched under the blankets, pulling her against me like a shield.

"Would you like to come over to my house tomorrow night?" she asked.

I almost said no. I wasn't ready to meet people or go through the pretense of smiling and listening to strangers. The lighthouse peered down, waves carousing as if understanding the beat of my heart. *Uh huh uh huh uh huh.* Susan reached behind her panties and scarfed up my pen, writing her address down on the cover of my notebook. The place was on Dune Road in Southampton, where I and all the other poor kids would drive to look at the rich houses we would never own or even be invited inside.

"Your house?" I asked.

"Yes. It's my birthday; I'm now officially nineteen."

I hated sounding inane, but I disliked being rude to a woman I'd been impotent with. "Happy birthday."

"Thank you."

The embarrassed grin again, and I pulled her closer. I was having a hard time keeping my eyes open. I was neither burning nor stoic. Somehow though, she fell asleep before me, in my arms as the rising sun began to burn away the mist, ashes of our campfire rustling across sand, and just before grogginess took hold and changed into something black and blissful, I noticed the thick, ugly scar weaving down the side of her throat.

C'mon.

2

When I woke up she was gone, and gorillas were smashing luggage inside my skull. For a wonderfully overpowering moment the night seemed only a particularly satisfying dream. There are times you manage to make it outside your own skin before being reeled back inside. It took a few seconds for my near perfect memory to fill in details, drawing them up one by one.

The seagulls *cawwed* relentlessly while an elderly couple of onlookers perused the beach, spotting pearlescent shells and pointing at odd rock formations, plucking up handfuls of baby sandcrabs.

I gathered my belongings and made a bee-line for my car, dreading the two-hour drive home. Reality set in. I sat resting my cheek against the steering wheel, stomach doing backflips. I looked at the address scrawled on my notebook, wondering whether I should go to Susan's party.

The headache was bad, but the rage remained furled. The drive back passed without my taking any great notice. When I got home I thought about little besides a hot shower and

doing more work on the book. I thought I could switch obses-
sions for a time. The story was coming together faster than
anything I'd written before, and I wanted to ride out the tentative streak for as long as I could.

Ulysses and Achilles gave me dirty looks when I opened
the door, but they didn't have time to lay on the guilt as they
raced into the backyard. I fed the dogs the leftover meatloaf
my mother couldn't get anyone else to eat, and had a couple
of cold slices of pizza that had aged worse than Hemingway
and Howard Hughes. My answering machine blinked four
times, and with some trepidation I hit the recall button. My
answering machine and I get along about as well as most
people got along with telegrams arriving at three AM.

The first message was Harrison, reminding me not to forget about meeting him for breakfast this morning. It was now
a quarter past twelve. The second call was a hang-up. So was
the third. And fourth.

Flopping back on the couch, the dogs swarmed me. Achilles' gray-white Husky face appeared more wolfish with meatloaf
hanging in his whiskers. Ulysses' slick, black Labrador fur
and puppy paws made him look more like a trained seal than
a guard dog. I missed Homer's basset hound snout shoved
against my neck, but I didn't miss his painfully arthritic whines
and awful cataract-glazed blind eyes.

In the end, Homer had stared at me as if I were my brother;
as I'd aged and begun to look more like D.B., Homer started
acting colder, promenading with an air of hatred. D.B. had
done a lot to the neighborhood dogs. Homer was the only
one to survive. The vet was forced to remove a kidney, rebuild
a number of ribs, and partially amputate three of his paws
and most of his ears.

I headed for the shower. Steaming jets of hot water cleaned off the last vestiges of salt and sand. I toweled down and dressed in black jeans and a white sweater, then checked the closet and found that both my suits were in appallingly bad taste for a birthday party on Dune Road.

Should I buy something more appropriate? Probably not, since I had no idea just what would be proper attire for a gathering in the Hamptons, and I didn't have the money, anyway. Odd memories jutted in sideways between thoughts of Linda and Susan: I recalled teenage jaunts when Harrison, Jack, and I had driven by the mansions like a carload of sharks and promised ourselves, *someday, someday.* I'd had a nagging suspicion even then that someday was tantamount to never.

The mail wasn't worth checking. Bills, two rejections on a couple of short stories, and one "maybe" from *Shamus* if I changed the ending of a novella and let the hero get the girl instead of discovering she was the serial killer he'd been chasing for twelve thousand words. I shucked it aside and stared out the blinds at nothing I wanted to see.

The phone rang.

It was Jack. He always sounded happy even after spending a double shift in the Seven Five busting dealers and clearing the street of drive-by shooting victims in Bedford Stuyvesant, the worst area of Brooklyn. I'd asked him his secret and he'd given me the book on efficient killing. It was officially outlawed by the police the same way switchblades were. Jack kept his knife strapped to his left ankle.

"Hey, buddy," he said. "What happened? Carrie told me that you and Linda broke up last night."

"You just answered your own question."

"Oh hell," he sighed. "I just know I don't have enough

liquor in the house. Just wait until you get antsy and claustophobic and go to take a ten-mile jog to clear your head but come staggering up my porch instead."

"Such faith."

"Remember what happened when you broke up with Dawn?"

"No," I answered honestly.

I'd awoken from a drunken blackout struggling with three male nurses in Bellvue's psychiatric wing. The doctors told me I'd broken into the dog pound and threatened to kill the employees. Only the fact that Jack had shown on the scene kept me out of jail.

"You can relax," I said. "This one's going to play out a little differently, I think."

I could imagine the spread of his smile. "Oh, and why's that? And don't say, 'don't ask' because I'm already asking. Why's that?"

"I've got a feeling."

"You had somebody else on the side?"

"No," I said.

"You met another woman *already*?"

"Not exactly. I'm not sure."

His voice shifted into something like a paternal tone, but with a tougher bite, on the verge of anger, but still too damn happy, ready to give orders. "You shouldn't have quit her, you know."

The wrinkle between my eyebrows grew deeper, my face reverting to a scowl; people outside the situation dropped advice into it like hand grenades down a manhole. The muscles in the corners of my jaw popped, and then my knees, and my neck. The headache dug in with barbed claws. "She gave me up." That was probably the truth.

My father barked in my mind. "*When they take your love and blood, take it back.*"

I heard Jack rubbing h.s beard stubble, enjoying this to some extent. "Well, okay. It's just that she's Carrie's best friend and I've known her for years and ... well, you know."

I didn't, but said, "Yeah."

"If you need to give me a call, you've got my number. I'll be on double shifts for the next two nights because of the riots in Bed-Sty. We'll talk later."

Of course we would. I worked on the book for an hour and, when the phone rang again, was surprised to see I'd written ten pages. I let the phone ring, allowing the machine to run interference while I broke Jacob Browning's leg and left him in an abandoned building with three hit men.

Then I remembered I'd shut the damn thing off after playing my messages. I swung out of my chair and picked up.

"Have you finished the climactic ending to *For Whom The Llama Tolls* or am I cutting you short?" Susan said.

I thought the shame of last night's failure would catch up to me when I heard her voice, but I was oddly elevated. "Hi," I said. I sounded more smitten than any guy ever wants to be caught being. "Perfect timing."

"I just wanted to make sure you were going to show up tonight, Nathaniel."

"Now, about that ..."

She snickered. "Let me guess. You're bugged because you have nothing to wear and you're afraid you'll look out of place brushing elbows with the rich folk, right?"

I never liked acumen, unless it was mine. "Something like that."

She was on a portable phone and walking too far away

from the unit. Heavy crackling tinged her words. "Tonight is
my night, filled with my friends and neighbors. So be comfortable. Come as you are. Loosen up and we'll have a fun
time, okay?"

"All right."

"Good. I'll expect you at around ... how's eight or there-
abouts?"

"Fine. Eight o'clock."

"I'll see you then."

The receiver hanging up was a bellow of thunder-filled
static.

***

I didn't know what to get a millionairess for her birthday, so
I tapped my bank account and bought her a dozen long-
stemmed white roses. At eight on the head I was driving down
Dune Road, staring at the mansions and the ninety-thou-
sand-dollar foreign cars lining the quarter-mile long imported
cobblestone driveways. I was painfully conscious that my black
suit, white shirt, and charcoal tie made me look more like a
member of the Moral Majority than someone who was loosened up and ready to have a fun time.

The Hartford home went beyond my *someday, someday* fan-
tasies and entered the realm of *King of Persia*. With its ocean-
front view and rows of windows and skylights, I wouldn't
have been too surprised to see either an Exxon tanker an-
chored off shore or Ben Hur racing by with his eight white
steeds. The mansion reeked of wealth and majesty. I smelled
like Old Spice.

The shame was catching up. Walking up to the house I
tried not to appear nervous and failed miserably; I repeatedly
switched the bouquet from hand to hand and wiped my wet

palms down the length of my pants legs. Susan met me at the door and something buzzed in the back of my brain. Had she actually been waiting for me?

"You look dashing," she said.

I muttered something incomprehensible; the lady who'd been cute and lovely in her own unintimidating way was now as awe-inspiring and erotic as any feverish fantasy my well of imagination could churn up. For someone who had told me to dress casually, Susan was in a high-collared black ballroom gown that exposed only her pale, china-doll hands; and yet, hidden away like that, she was even sexier than a stripper lathered in oil. She knew it, too. She fit perfectly within the frame of the large doorway to her own home.

I held the roses out straight-armed the way a bashful kid on his first date will offer a corsage. I managed to say, "You are absolutely ... enchanting." It was a word a writer should use. At any other time it would have sounded false, stupid, or hopelessly outdated; but here on her veranda, spoken to her as she gazed at me as she'd done on the beach, her features still cut from the shadows of night, "enchanting" was all I could say. Besides "Happy birthday."

"Thank you, Nathaniel." She took the bouquet and brought it to her face, breathing in the fragrance while I continued staring. Almost sadly she said, "You're so thoughtful." She reached for my hand and led me inside, and the world surrounding me—in that same moment, from the first step to the second—went from something stunning and radiant to something just south of Soddom and Gomorrah.

Most of her friends had taken her up on her word to come as they were and act naturally—some of their natures leaned more towards the reptile cage than high society. I even recognized two or three of the bikers who were drunkenly dueling with shish-kabob.

Once, after drinking with Jack, we left a bar to discover that somebody had stomped my car's windshield and crushed in the hood; the guy's footprints were visible in the scraped paint. At the far end of the parking lot a man gave me the finger, hopped into a red truck, and tore ass out of there. I went back inside the bar and asked if anybody knew a dude who wore workboots and drove a red pick-up. A bunch of people coughed up his name because drunks don't think about consequences, they like to talk. I tracked the guy to his house, slashed his tires, and smashed in his windshield. I'd have given anything to see the look on his face when he realized that poetic justice had caught up with him.

The guy with the workboots was here, chugging a stein of ale in the corner with a flame-haired woman whose breasts did not entirely fit into her T-shirt. Two girls in mini-skirts were groping each other on a divan. A man with a tattoo of a spider-web that stretched across his neck and up his left cheek was eating caviar and sucking on a bottle of champagne; he laughed and sputtered over himself.

The stench was overpowering, and I couldn't quite keep from gagging. Susan walked me across the room. Pockets of smoke hung in the air like gray balloons. The pungent odors of expensive perfumes mixed with the marijuana, burned meat, and the white roses. Loud, indecipherable voices rose above the music. The cool, steering touch of Susan rested on my wrist.

And yet, for certain—as I was taken and spun by the stale heat of bodies—there were diamond tiaras and tuxedos to be seen at every angle. Cliques were formed back-to-back: pearls and four-carat pinkie rings sidled against safety-pin speared noses. My instincts took firmer hold, and I started drawing up furious scenes of confrontation, though there were none.

A woman in a silk dress kissed me and said, "Antoine, how good it is to see you again—give mummy all my love." I assured her I would. In the moving mass of two hundred people there appeared to be an equal split between children of tycoons and the children of street people.

"Where are your mother and father?" I asked, about as nonchalant as a parish priest.

"They're on a business trip to Egypt right now. Or maybe they've already left for their vacation to the Riviera." She backed up a step and stared at me, the burning stoic. "Do you think it's just another case of self-centered, uncaring parents?" I did, but said nothing. She read me, anyway, and smiled. "That's not the case, Nathaniel. My father can be a little on the tough side, but they're great people. Their business trips take them all over the world. There are season-long gaps when we're not even on the same hemisphere. That's their lifestyle. I learned to live with it a long time ago."

My acumen was off.

"C'mon," she said, "lets go to the bar."

C'mon.

I'd get it back. I shut up. As we walked to get the drinks, a woman slightly older than Susan sidled up and threw an arm around her shoulder, leaning over and whispering in her ear.

"Nathaniel Follows, I'd like for you to meet my sister, Jordan."

The woman made a flamboyant but graceful curtsy that showed enough thigh through her slit skirt to restart the Trojan war; it took a few seconds to see they were related because the physical differences between her and Susan were extreme upon first meeting.

Where Susan was petite, Jordan Hartford was built like an
athlete and nearly as tall as my own five feet eleven inches.
Her wild, California-blond dye job cascaded down in a jumble
of intricate braids. After I got over the obvious differences, I
could make out their similar features; Jordan's seemed accented at every turn, sharper, thinner, with carefully placed
make-up to pronounce each individual angle of her face, like
a crystal figurine. "How do you do, Nathaniel."

"Hello, Jordan." I took her hand. She held it out to me as
though I should kiss it, so I did.

"Susan tells me you're an aspiring novelist."

I shrugged. "I gave up most of my aspirations when I saw
the size of my first royalty check."

She tittered happily at that. Unlike her sister, Jordan's giggle
worked on my nerves like a dentist's drill. "Tell me the truth
though: are you trying to be the next James Joyce, a literary
genius, or the next Stephen King?"

I didn't want to talk about it. Nobody who waits for checks
in the mail ever wants to talk about it. I rocked on my heels.
"I decided a while back that I'd try to be the first Nathaniel
Follows."

She pursed her lips. "Hmm. Quite honest."

Merely inane. People like to hear that standard response
from authors because it makes them feel as though they are
still patrons of the arts. "Hmm. Quite. But if I had my choice
I'd go for the big bucks. Unfortunately, I've discovered, it's
not my choice."

Susan smiled prettily, but there was a growl tainting her
tone. "Does he pass your regimen of tests, Jordan? Or shall
we toss him back into the ocean?" I could almost see her
own rage slithering up the back of her neck, peering at me
over her shoulder.

"I'm just saying hello, for chrissakes. Don't get all uppity."

"I am most certainly," Susan stated with cool emphasis, "not *uppity*."

Jordan's dimples flashed as her smile crinkled in at one end; she had that air about her which only the extremely self-confident and gun owners have. My brother had it too, even at the end, even in the morgue. Electricity seemed to snap between the sisters. My nape bristled. Sibling rivalry was a commodity the rich did not lack, and I felt sad that for a birthday girl who would someday inherit millions of dollars, Susan did not look very happy.

"Enjoy the party," Jordan told me, and her hand came up to brush back my hair in a friendly gesture. I swallowed thickly. She escaped into the throng.

Susan clapped a tumbler into my hand and introduced me to a swarm of people rank with the sweet stink of marijuana. I slammed the drink back without tasting it and she replaced the empty glass. "You've got some catching up to do," she said, urging me to knock the second down quickly too. I did. And a third. They were Martinis. The fourth was wine, and I sipped it slowly.

Holding me by the elbow, Susan moved into the herd, forcing me to say hello to people who went by names no less memorable than Gregory Artemis III and his fiancee Heather Ann Linsington-all-the-way-from-England, both of whom were wide-eyed as guppies and asked my opinion on the realities of the Soviet break-up; there was Poo-bah Pete, Teddy B. Kerryson, Gotta-lot Lisa, Silvermouth, Prince Primavera and his sister the Princess Panegyric, neither of whom appeared to be breathing, and plain ol' John, who rushed away without shaking my hand.

Linda's mouth was everywhere.

A hand tapped my shoulder, and I wheeled around. Zenith Brite sang in a local band whom I'd seen perform several times over the past couple of years—I enjoyed her slow and sad bluesey songs. She told me she'd be playing The Bridge and asked me to stop in sometime during the week; I decided I would. Behind her stood Fat Ernie, and Fatter Ernie—who carried a sleeping kitten more tenderly than I've ever been touched—and Fattest-Ernie-Of-Them-All, who weighed more than the other two combined. He sipped a Diet Coke and chatted about St. Thomas Aquinas with such intelligence and passion that nearby conversations broke up and a crowd began to form around him.

Even though nothing had been said outright, I still felt that Susan considered me her escort for the evening. I realized that for the past fifteen minutes I'd been unconsciously doing my best to memorize as many faces as I could. I noticed people were giving me steely-eyed glances. They were trying to commit my face to memory, as well. It seemed a lot of enemies were being made, but I didn't know why.

"I'll be back in a minute," Susan said. It was the first thing she'd said all night to make me feel as though I shouldn't be inseparably knitted to her side.

She stopped and talked to others, most of whom she seemed to be meeting for the first time; maybe they were casual acquaintances or just friends of Jordan's. She walked in that scurrying line hostesses often do when they have so many guests and are compelled to chat half a minute with each of them. She weaved in and out. By the time she was halfway across the room I saw something in her fist for a moment, and then it was gone. Nice sleight of hand. I pride myself on

being observant, but hadn't seen where she'd picked up the
bag of cocaine.

I regarded a row of faces in the area she'd wandered past.
I probably wouldn't have bothered if I wasn't already feeling
somewhat drunk and invincible. D.B. had sold coke for years
before the police found him. It was reminiscent of the time he
was killing children.

Uh huh, uh huh, come on.

I blocked the dead children, who suddenly wanted to talk.
We had a lot to catch up on. The headache left in an instant.
I stared at the group: they all had the same swarthy belliger-
ence about them, except for the man in the middle, around
whom the rest huddled. He looked back, his mouth twisted
into an oddly polite sneer of a smile as he watched me intently. He had the whitest, sharpest teeth I'd ever seen on a
human being; one of the few things in the room that flashed
even more brightly than his smile was the ruby tie-pin that
shined off his chest. He must have gone on a lot of lucrative
business trips south of the border. Although he was small, the
peddler had the aura of a bully. There was something about
him I almost liked.

A no-neck bouncer type noticed our staring match and
whispered in the peddler's ear. The peddler made a brush-off
gesture; I was nobody.

"Where'd you get the coke?" I asked, when Susan returned.
The children giggled distantly. The aloof glance she gave me
proved I didn't quite sound as uninterested as I'd hoped. She
ignored the question and sauntered off, and I followed like a
pup. The wine was gone and, although things weren't spinning, they had a nice bend to them. We wandered past the
lady in the silk dress, and she threw me kisses and called out,

"Adieu, Antoine, never forget our weekend in Marseilles!" I promised her I wouldn't.

The tour Susan gave me through the halls and up the stairways seemed twice as long as it probably was. Before I realized we were out of the thick of the horde, I was standing in her bedroom, looking at a host of stuffed animals that yawned up at me from her four-poster bed.

Without appearing too uncomfortable in her gown, she drifted over and leaned against one of the bedposts. "Is it strange to you?"

"What do you mean?"

"Tonight. This. Everything."

"Oh," I said. "Everything. Well, since you put it that way ..."

She grinned. "You know what I mean."

Maybe I did. Everything was pretty strange and, for the most part, always had been. She wanted an easy answer to a redundant question. "I'm a writer. I take each new situation, encounter, and occasion as a valuable experience and channel it into the ongoing entirety of my life's work."

"Bullshit," she said.

"Okay, so it's bullshit."

"Why's it got to mean anything?"

"Why ask me?"

"Because you know something," she said, suddenly so intense and serious I withdrew a step.

We frowned at each other; rhetoric owned the room, and we were both talking too cryptically. She stood nose to nose with me, pressing against me gently, gazing into my eyes as if they fell twelve feet backwards into my brain's murky waters. It made me feel like I wasn't there. I held her face in my hands, forcing her to focus on me again.

I said, "Because you were out on the Point last night with me. I had a personal reason to freeze my ass off; you must have had one, too."

"Maybe," she laughed. Her smile crinked up parentheses around her mouth, not quite her sister's dimples. She breathed deeply and slowly, and when she brushed her lips against mine I saw something back down behind her eyes. "Is your forty-eight hour mourning period over yet, Nathaniel? Are we ready to try again?"

"Yes," I said.

"Good." She reached for my belt. "I want you to fuck me. I like it in the dark and I like it rough. I want you to fuck me until we can't walk anymore."

That was okay with me.

***

There was nothing else besides our black anger and the moist bitterness, nipping and gnawing, and the out-of-breath pleasure. She had me. I felt had. I made her have me. I took her. We switched rages and fucked them, too.

The darkness stole away reality. I couldn't see her face, and being drunk didn't help to pull any of it together. Maybe she was counting on that to get me in a rough mood. When I tried to kiss her she bit my neck, drawing blood, sucking hard, tongue probing. She was sweaty and slippery, and I knew that all evening she'd been horribly uncomfortable and hot in her heavy dress.

"Dig it in," she commanded. "C'mon, stuff it in. Dig me."

I dug her.

I bit her lips in answer before peeling her vulva apart and driving into her. She set the speed at a dangerous level, burning, out of control. It didn't happen like this often. I slid out several times when she cut left when I was cutting right, but we found a rhythm and kept it going. I wouldn't want to walk for a week. We were both abandoned, and abandoned each other. She growled, pissed off, and groaned painfully, begging with each thrust. I loved the sound of her cries, and laughed in her face while she wept. It fed, yet eased, the shame. I pounded her with misplaced fury, tasting her, chewing on the soft hairs below her ear. She reached around, clawed my back, and kept fighting me off whenever I tried to run my hands over the rest of her body. She wanted my teeth. It's difficult to screw someone who wants to be smothered, but doesn't want to be touched.

There were scars besides the puckered one running down her neck—thin and curved. Others felt broad and high-ridged. Beneath the animosity I thought *car accident, shattered windshield*. In our frenzy we didn't care. I didn't care. I was a dog.

She pushed me off and turned over, guiding me inside from behind. She grunted and mewled each inch, and I kept working it from there. *Uh huh uh huh*. She came and rode the curve through two more orgasms. I couldn't think; I couldn't form words. The darkness became our blackness released. She liked it hard and fast, and when she fell flat on her belly and let me hammer away, I thought I'd bleed to death from all the tiny tortures that had been cutting for so long. When I came I wasn't even sure if she was there anymore.

***

Susan dressed in stinging darkness without saying a word. There was no cuddling, no quiet talk, no wasted efforts on tenderness now that the act was complete. My shame was gone. Her movements were slow and wary beside me, as though she were afraid I might yank her back under the covers, or worse, try to caress her. Instead, I laid in bed dissecting my feelings; nothing for certain came to mind. The silence between us grew in her black bedroom until, finally, she turned on the light.

"You were good," she said.

Something had been incredibly fulfilling about our hatemaking—the slipstream rush and grinding, the painful charge, nails dug in muscle. A lot had been left out; I'd wanted it that way. She hadn't, even though she'd egged me on, pretending love never stood a chance. Her sweat clung to me like the missing pieces of our sex.

I put on my clothes, and we walked out. Much of the party had moved onto the third floor, and through the skylights I saw stars. A thousand empty sentences came to mind, but I was too embarrassed to speak. Susan smiled to her guests but went by without saying anything to anyone. She lifted the hem of her dress and fanned herself with it.

"Christ, it's hot."

"It is warm in here with everybody," I said. "But I thought most houses this close to the shore were shut up for the winter."

"Jordan and I will be leaving for Miami next Friday." A smile nicked the corner of her mouth. "This latch is stuck. Can you get it?"

The window was twice the size of a person and rolled out to open at an angle; directly below were a couple of chaise lounges set under a giant umbrella on a patio larger than most basketball courts. "Why don't we just go and sit outside?" I offered.

Susan's lips flattened and the lights of her eyes danced

angrily; it was faked. She play-acted as if she wanted to stick around with the rest of the group in case I had notions our fucking meant more than it was; I knew what it meant and she knew I knew. It was clear she wanted me to impress her with romance, but she wouldn't accept any form of friendship. I had wanted to touch her, and she hadn't let me. We had no real meeting place beyond the rage.

"What's that look for?" I asked.

"It's hot."

"Susan ..."

"Please," she said. "Open this damn window."

Other windows beside us were cracked open a few inches. I grabbed the latch and tugged, but the thing wouldn't budge. I yanked again and still nothing. I felt like I was breaking into a crypt. I tried again and my biceps swelled against my shirt; I'd torn a fingernail on Susan's thigh and the pain flashed up my arm. My back burned from gouges. I pulled. This time the window glided open perfectly.

"Thanks." She stretched in the breeze and let her hair waft about her. "That's a lot better."

Somebody threw an arm around my waist. Jordan's perfume made me sneeze as she pulled me aside with a knowing, but idiotic grin. "So, how was it between you two carnivores?"

"Bloody," I said.

I tried to get away but she was drunk and kept tugging me and tugging me, crooning in my ear. The perfume was disgusting and drained my sinuses. I went into a coughing jag and looked back at Susan watching the two of us wrestling.

Her mouth silently formed the word, 'Bye.

And I knew.

It was obvious what she was going to do. Jumbled fragments in my mind snapped together with the audible mental click of tumblers turning to a correct combination. Strangely enough, I felt an incredible sense of relief, a weight falling from my shoulders now that I understood my role on her stage; our fucking had been one last chance to pass the test of the living, one final search for love, or only acceptance, and we'd failed each other miserably. My God. I could still hear the way her voice sounded when she'd whispered last night, *Death is everywhere.* Where else would it be? I'd brought it to her.

She winked at me as she moved closer to the moon. Did she want me to follow? I would have wanted her with me if I'd been leading the dance. But I wasn't. I needed her more than ever. It all came together like a mirror reflecting a face of quiet agony.

Jordan was still holding on to me, tittering and asking for graphic details; she cried out as I batted her away. I rushed at Susan, dove, and almost grabbed her ankle as she took a step forward. But Fatter Ernie got in the way, hugging and speaking softly to his sleepy kitten, and I floundered over his leg. I stretched wildly, but only got a piece of Susan's dress with my fingertips as she walked out through the open window. She didn't scream.

In fact, she was smiling.

It was me who screamed.

3

Laid out on the floor I hyper-extended myself, continuing to reach, hearing the windy whoosh of her long hair splayed out behind her as she dropped, even as I screamed. I craned my neck and peered over the edge of the sill, and caught the unfolding last half-second of the life of Susan Hartford.

It was beautiful to watch in its own way. It was a convergence of every lost love I'd let die. Thirty-two feet per second^2, the rate at which objects fall: bowling balls, anemic businessmen, beautiful ladies. To the trained observer, to a man always searching for a story inside the dark, the final fraction of his momentary lover's life played out with a startling grace unlike anything he'd witnessed before. The patio spotlights focused on her swan song.

It was searing, as all desperate escapes are: Susan's dress was too tight on her body; the rage clung between her breasts; she seemed to be arcing in control of her flight, the smile affixed; her arms stretched overhead, pointed down and diving.

The scratches on my back, and the teeth gouges, began bleeding again as I tried to make eye contact with her. Curls whipped past her face, strands waving beneath her nostrils, nudged by her last breath. Her left shoe shrugged free from her foot, slipping and turning away heel over toe as if attempting to evade her fate. Each piece of the scene took on a life of its own, and a death. Images trapped in a shattered mirror, raining down thirty-two feet per second^2. For eternity.

If she'd gone through any other window she might have lived. She'd thought it through, good girl; if you were going to do it, do it for real. No mere attention-getter here, no hope of being saved when you choose a thirty foot drop onto cement. She might even have purposefully turned in mid-air like a cat, aiming to spike herself on the point of the porch umbrella. She struck it hard. Alhough the tip wasn't sharp enough to impale her, I could tell by the explosion of blood that her rib-cage had smashed up through her heart. She hung there balanced at the top of the metal pole for an instant, then toppled onto the patio table beneath. The force of her fall scattered the chaise lounges.

I threw up.

I couldn't stop, everything came free from today, yesterday, Linda's last meal, the grit and salt of the Point. It came from the very bottom. There was blackness in there, and more than a little red. I got to my knees and managed to stand. Slowly I became aware of noises behind me, people running and crowding the window, the furniture toppling and bottles thumping on the carpet. The room filled with a buzzing like flies. I was transfixed at my station, growling, maybe mewling. I couldn't make much of it out. Leaning forward, I braced myself against the sill, wavering as I saw the valet parking attendants gaping at Susan's broken form.

Steadily, the sounds became more distinct as the pound-

ing of my pulse slowed in my ears. Jordan was gasping beside
me, taking hesitant steps to the window, one hand seeking
purchase on my shoulder but not quite touching me, the other
outstretched to the night as if she might be next to pitch
herself through. The annoying distant voice behind me grew
louder, repeating and becoming clearer.

Fatter Ernie was shouting. His kitten looked at me suspi-
ciously.

"That guy pushed her! I saw him push Susan!" Fatter Ernie
shoved his cat at me, pointing me out. "Him! I saw him! He
pushed her!"

***

Jordan's eyes crossed and she passed out in my arms. Fatter
Ernie made a rush towards me and I staved him off with a
glance that told him I'd make him swallow his cat if he came
any closer. He didn't. I wished he had. There was an eruption
of girls weeping and shrieking when they realized what had
happened—a rush towards the other windows, holding themselves firmly against the glass, afraid to move and afraid not
to move, peering at the illuminated wreckage.

People shouted and ran in a dozen different directions,
scrambling down the stairways. Several toilets flushed at the
same time, and then once again. Prince Primavera towed his
sister through the hallway like a deaf-mute begger. Gotta-lot
Lisa took a peek out the window and made faces of fascinated disgust.

The guy with the commonplace name of John, who'd
dashed off earlier without shaking my hand, stared at me. His
eyes narrowed, but his thick glasses still made them seem too
wide. He might actually believe I'd shoved Susan out the win-

dow, especially now that I was holding an unconscious Jordan, as though I might throw her to her death as well.

Small and wiry, he scuttled forward. The top half of his head was so magnified that his face was all eyes, like an insect. He stood six feet away without revealing any emotion, except for a tear, or maybe a bead of sweat, that slid down his face. When I told him to call an ambulance he merely hunched his shoulders and dizzily walked off towards Susan's bedroom.

I hefted Jordan and brought her downstairs to a couch in the living room. The first wails of sirens could be heard at the entrance of Dune Road.

The state of confusion on the first floor was no better than upstairs, but at least the bluebloods clung together in tenth-generation cliques; the glass doors to the patio were open and plugged with paling voyeurs. One of the Brits was trembling and kept missing his mouth with his champagne glass. In a brittle voice he said, "'Ow 'orrible. My god ... ghastly." Ladies wept in the arms of their fiancés, and the men rubbed their backs and spoke meaningless words.

I lifted Jordan's eyelids but didn't know what the hell I was checking for. The bathroom was locked, so I kicked it in and discovered two girls huddled around the bowl flushing baggies of coke and pot. They looked at me like deer caught in the glare of headlights. My brother's favorite type: pony-tails, halter tops, pixiish features, and small tits.

I wet a towel and returned to Jordan's side. Cold compresses didn't wake her, and after a minute of rubbing her wrists and washing her face I started to get worried. Finally, as the cops came in, she began to rouse.

Heading the group of police, entering the house like a wedge, was a powerfully-built, impeccably-dressed officer with red-rimmed, tired eyes. He gave sharp orders to the uniformed cops, glanced around the room looking past faces until he saw Jordan. He came over and flashed his badge and identification at me: LIEUTENANT DANIEL SMITHFIELD.

"Is Miss Hartford hurt?" he asked.

"No," I answered, thinking, *not this one*, surprised he would know her on sight. "She's fainted."

"Who are you?"

"My name's Nathaniel Follows."

D.B., and subsequently my father, had gotten plenty of coverage after the back yard was dug up. It had been fourteen years ago, but that kind of Americana lived on in the neighborhoods. The made-for-TV movie showed up now and again on Sunday afternoons. I scanned his eyes; if he knew the name Follows, he didn't show it.

"Did you see what happened here?"

"Yes."

He ran a hand over his face, looked down at her, and called one of his men. "Bring smelling salts."

Smithfield sat on the edge of the couch and held Jordan's wrist, checking her pulse as she moaned; it was a husky sound, reminding me of her sister. He took the towel from my hand and made a casual pass with it over Jordan's face.

"All right, Follows. I don't know what your action is or what happened here yet, so don't move. If you move I'll have to run after you, except I don't run after anybody. I'm too slow. Bad knees from the tunnels in 'Nam. Hell of a marksman, though. We do understand each other?"

He didn't look old enough to have been in Vietnam, but he made his point and deserved something for his dramatic flair. "Yes," I said.

Uh huh, uhmm hm.

Smithfield turned away. He was obviously familiar with a number of people who'd been too drunk or wasted to make it out the front door. He motioned for the uniformed officers to get them out of there. To others—like Princess Panegyric—he acted personable and friendly, addressing them with an elaborate politeness; as par for the entire evening, I had the distinct feeling I was out of my element. All three of the Ernies clustered around Smithfield and spoke in hushed voices, gesturing in my direction.

Jordan's body tensed and her hands flashed out the way they do when you feel like you're falling out of bed. The other cop came back with the smelling salts, but left when he saw she was awakening. Jordan's eyes fluttered open. She focused on me and then beyond me on the police.

"Who?"

"Shhh, it's okay."

She stared at me for a long time without saying anything. A bruise was rising on her cheek from where I'd smacked her trying to get to the window. Carefully touching her face with the wet towel, I washed off more make-up; without eyeliner and painted-in high cheekbones she was nearly Susan's twin. Even the wild California-blond hair, having lost some of its moussed hold, was less a personal style than a way to appear different from her sister.

"She's dead, isn't she?"

"Yes."

"Of course she is."

"Of course," I echoed.

Her voice cracked with exertion as she fought for control, lost it, regained it. The tears came, and she silently sobbed,

every muscle in her face taut as a witch's. It went on like that
for a minute until she broke through whatever wall she was
pressed against. Her face uncontorted, each line becoming
smooth as silk, eyes blazing as she went into a talking jag.

"I looked down and there she was covered with blood, the
patio fucked-up, the dress ruined. My dress, of course, she
had to borrow my dress like she doesn't own anything herself.
The first thing I thought was, like, *Ah hell*, shit, now that was
a stupid thing to do. It was. It really was. Like that? You do it
like that? On the patio? On your birthday? In my dress?"
Jordan snapped her jaws together, her teeth clacking loudly. I
winced. "Bloody. You said bloody. I can smell it on you." Her
chest heaved. "What happened, Nathaniel?" There was a trap
in her voice, an accusation. "Tell me. And I don't just mean
right then, I mean what the hell happened between the two of
you?" Her nails came up, ready for my eyes. "Tell me. What
did you do to her?"

"We made love," I said.

The children, or my brother, laughed. My breathing hitched
in my throat. Love was a bad word to use; I knew better. I'd
called it hatemaking myself. If we had attempted anything
else, if either of us had had what it took to make love, perhaps
she wouldn't have jumped; perhaps, instead, I would have.

Jordan bolted upright and shoved me away. "Jesus, is she
gone? Did they take my sister away?"

"No, not yet. Not for a while."

"I've got to see her."

"Maybe you shouldn't, Jordan."

She was already moving. Smithfield met her halfway to
the patio doors and took her aside, showing a great deal of
respect. She nodded and brushed past him while he sadly

watched her go by. He had two personas—the hard-ass and the light touch; the lieutenant shifted into them with equal ease, back and forth, even as he crossed the room to me.

Fatter Ernie was getting louder in the corner. "But, Officer, he pushed her! I saw it! I'll sign anything you want me to. I mean, do your duty and arrest that guy!"

I said, "If you keep squawking like that I'm going to hit you very hard and send you to the hospital."

Fatter Ernie blanched and held his cat up like a crucifix to ward me away. "You all heard him. Now he's threatening me, Officer!"

"Name," Smithfield said.

"Nathaniel Follows," I repeated.

"Address. Occupation."

I told him.

"You were her date tonight?"

"Something like that."

"You either were or you weren't."

"That's not exactly true."

Smithfield's chin dropped to his chest and he pursed his lips. He looked as if he would very much enjoy kicking me in the balls. "You going to give me rhetoric?"

I was surprised he knew the word *rhetoric*. "We met only last night. She invited me to her birthday party and the two of us spent most of the night together. Yes, I suppose I was her date."

"Tell me everything that happened."

I told him most of it; I left out the trying on of each other's pain, and I didn't mention the bag she'd picked up from the peddler. When I got to the part where she mouthed the word, *"Bye,"* he said, "No one else heard her say that."

"She didn't say it—she mouthed it."

"You were close enough to push her."

"No, I wasn't. I had to make a dash over Fatter Ernie's love handles to even get near her, but I was too late."

"Several witnesses say you opened the window."

"She asked me to."

"Did she ask you to push her?"

I took a deep breath. "I think you should file that one under 'obtuse.'"

He plowed ahead. "So you admit you had sex with her. Maybe it wasn't consensual. Maybe you raped her, then shoved her out the window because you were scared."

"No," I said.

He shrugged and said, "Maybe," as though I should take a couple minutes to think it over.

"Are we through?"

"Yeah, Follows, I guess we are. For now. We'll have more questions later." I knew they would; somebody was bound to run a cross-check and confuse me with my father.

The wind whipped leaves against the windows, scratching against the glass like Susan trying to get at my back again. I pressed my way through the remaining group of people who turned aside and talked quietly among themselves, waiting for the police to finish taking statements. There was some nervous laughter. As if it were established and expected, I took my place beside Jordan while the EMTs lifted Susan's body onto a gurney and took her away.

Vivisected like hounds, there were so many emotions within me cut out and laid open I couldn't feel anything. Listening to the ocean beating the beach a hundred yards distant, I thought how right Susan had been to say death was everywhere. She had proved it.

Lieutenant Smithfield came up beside me and shook his head. "Not even Halloween yet," he sighed. "Shit. It's gonna be a hell of an October."

***

Without saying anything more to Jordan I left, drove home but couldn't sleep, and tossed in the confines of the dark, missing the touch of Susan's body; when dawn arrived I was grateful for light. I walked the dogs and jogged the mile to the cemetery.

Sitting on my father's grave, I plucked off dry, brown petals that drifted over from neighboring plots, and stared at my name on the tombstone. I felt vaguely ghost-like, resurrected. I wondered where Susan would be buried, and whether anybody had been in touch with her parents yet.

No other visitors were in sight. My father's damned soul frolicked with my rage and the dogs out on the expanse of lawn. I could hear the dead children singing Catholic school prayers. I couldn't help but compare my father's drawn-out cancerous agony to D.B.'s dissected victims and Susan's quick kill. In my mind I saw the scars covering her flesh that I'd really only felt while we sweated, and I thought of shattered glass, surgery, and knives.

My father had known what my brother was doing and perhaps even helped him; the police never proved it in court, but they had come damn close. He'd watched D.B. burying the children in the back yard, I was as sure of it as everyone else. I'd always carry that certainty.

Susan Hartford knew I would also carry her rage, coupled to my own. I gave her a great deal of credit in the study of Nathaniel Follows. Out at Montauk, she'd listened to me spill my guts about everything from Mom's waffles to unrequited love, and she had understood my vulnerability, my quest for mystery. She didn't know about my need for redemption, but she'd discovered the truth in my impotence.

Playing me perfectly in a handful of hours, crying on my chest and loving a stranger, fucking the fury, she'd proven my inherent aggression. Did she rely on my misplaced guilt to propel me on a hunt through her life? Did she know my name? Did she watch the made-for-TV movie and realize the child actor playing me didn't have the right amount of crow's feet around his eyes? That the scene of the torn-up backyard didn't contain enough bodies?

She understood I would follow through on her finale. Susan had drawn me into her death like hooking a fish.

"Christ," I whispered.

I spun and gripped the gravestone, pounding the top of it with my fists; the stone was as cold as the rocks where she and I met. How could she have *done this to me?*

I cursed the precision of my memory, knowing I wouldn't forget even the smallest detail of the party, our sex, every touch and thrust and bite, each frame of her death. The pictures would never blur, the sharpened edges of my feelings would never erode. I'd had fourteen years to live down my brother's insanity, and a decade to live down my father's death, and still they haunted me. She knew I was a man who would never let go. She expected me to do a final favor for her, and knew I wouldn't be able to quit until I discovered and finished whatever it was.

I leaned back against my father's tombstone, watching him have fun with my own madness, and damned her to hell.

4

The next day, I stopped by my friend Harrison's place on my morning jog and the two of us went for a run in the park. In an effort to make up for my missing our breakfast meeting yesterday, I'd given him a call at 7:00 AM. Harrison was always awake by seven so he could fit a few hours of writing in before his security guard job began at noon.

He sensed something was wrong immediately. He didn't push; he was the only one who never pushed. I gave him the lowdown on the Linda split, but we'd been friends long enough for him to realize there was something else. He fixed his gaze on the ground, and where the trail thinned so we couldn't run side by side, he led me through the woods. I kept quiet for as long as I could, safe in his understanding.

Short stories were his forte. He'd gotten a small bite at notoriety when *Murderzone* published his novelette "Reaching For Your Spleen." The editors received more letters over his tale than anything published before.

For five years Harrison had been rewriting a thousand-page manuscript fictionalizing the life of Edgar Allan Poe. I'd read most of it back in college, at least most of the original book before he'd changed sections of it over and over, searching for a perfection he'd never find. I didn't like the novel; he'd used bits and pieces of what he'd learned about my brother: Poe chewed dogs and abused children. Poe maimed the raven and heartlessly murdered poor lost Lenore.

Two women with baby carriages gave us the eye as we cut clear of the trail and across the playground field. There was no mistaking Harrison. At six five he weighed two hundred pounds of solidly packed muscle, and moved with as pure a motion as a charging grizzly. If his powerful fluidity wasn't enough to gain him a second glance, the silver-tinged waves of his flowing black hair and thick beard would be. He resembled a taller, slightly saner Charles Manson. He didn't especially appreciate such analogies although he agreed with them.

We broke our third mile and hadn't exchanged ten words. His patience far exceeded mine. I was breathing hard by the time we got to the cage of the basketball courts, but I wanted to talk. Harrison knew it and lifted his gaze. He slowed to a stop and looked at me.

"You wanna talk?"

"No," I said. Cover up, common reaction. Then, "I don't know."

"Okay." He wandered the court, unwinding, stretching. Like a dancer, or a dancing bear, he carried an atmosphere of balance about himself. He was dressed for comfort in a baggy green and white sweatshirt and a pair of faded gray sweatpants that were wearing thin at the knees and cuffs. "The break with Linda putting you through the grinder?"

"No."

"Okay."

"There's more to it than that. This might take a while."

He shrugged and leaned back against the cage, looking at the empty courts. "Understandable."

"What do you mean?" I asked, but he said nothing else.

I climbed to the top of the fence and sat perched like a crow. He rested below me and listened while I told him about Susan Hartford from the beginning, leaving out no detail, leaving it complete rather than the edited version I'd told Smithfield. After a while I wasn't talking to Harrison anymore, but to her, perhaps, or to myself. It took an hour. Harrison never said a word. Drops of sweat slipped down my back and pooled at the base of my spine.

The ladies with the baby carriages were gone. The wind cooled my burning back; a couple of the deepest scratches were already infected. Dogs barked in the distance.

"That it?" Harrison finally asked.

I tried to think if there was anything more, if I should mention anything he might find interesting enough to put in his Poe book.

I kept silent. He stroked his chin, plucking at the black and silver hairs, smoothing them into place. "You feel caught up in it."

"Yes," I admitted.

"I would, too," he said. "Was she a good lay?"

"Yes. Didn't I say that?"

"No, you broke it down into details, but said nothing of what you felt."

"It was good."

"But was she good?"

"We were good."

He frowned as if I'd been caught in a lie. "I should think

so. That's when it works best, when you work best with yourself, inside. You ever been fucked like that before?"

"No."

"Never happened to me." He stroked his beard like a beloved pet. "It's over you know."

"No," I said, "it's not."

"Yes, it is. Nothing's going to help you from this point
on. Whatever you think you feel for her, you're truly only
feeling for yourself. She's not in a position to give anything
back. Whatever you're throwing into this, you're throwing
away. You're going to hate her, if you don't already. Are you
prepared to deal with that in the end? When you finally figure out you've been alone the whole time?"

"Not much different from the way things are now, anyway," I said.

"So you'll spawn upstream. You're going to swim back to
the beginning." He sighed like an overindulgent parent, as if
he had all the experience in the world but was ready to let me
make my own mistakes. "You gonna start with the smiley guy
you called the Peddler?"

"I don't know."

"Do you have any idea what his real name is?"

"No."

"Why don't you ask Jordan?"

"I don't want to have to go that route. Not yet, anyway.
There are other considerations. She just lost her sister. I'm at
least part of the reason. There's a bruise on her face. She's
alone, without even the benefit of having her parents bear
some of the brunt. She's in her own hell right now, and I
don't want to add to the burden."

"Why not?" Harrison said. "Defenses are low, you might

save yourself a lot of time and trouble. You could tumble to all your answers in the first shot. She might tell you every-thing you need to know. What you want to hear."

He was right, but I didn't want to face Jordan yet, until I was sure she was back in make-up and didn't look so much like her sister.

I could almost hear the circuits of Harrison's brain open-ing and closing, the Poe book subtly shifting sentence from sentence. He asked, "Have you told Jack about any of this? You might want a cop in your corner in case this Lieutenant Smithfield decides he wants to break chops."

"Jack's busy with trouble in Bed-Sty, and there's little enough love lost between NYPD and the Suffolk cops."

He grinned without actually smiling. "'Little love lost.' You must be a novelist. I get goose-bumps when you make words sing like that." He stood and turned, looking out at the parents playing soccer with their kids in the field. "She left a dare in the air behind her when she went out the window. For you or for anyone?"

"For me," I said.

"I wonder if she knew what she was doing, or if she just happened to meet the perfect guy to stumble over her pain. Maybe she was sitting out on that beach for months, reject-ing others, waiting for you." She would have waited. She had enough faith to make the effort. "You got a hunch? Or do you want to hear mine?"

"I've got one."

"Okay." He shook his head slowly, same non-smile lurk-ing beneath the thickness of his beard. "You might not find anything. Or you might find something you don't want to. You're going to lose either way, Nathaniel. It's just a matter of how much you give away to her."

I nodded.

"What are you going to do?" he asked.

"Push and see what happens."

"Someone might push back."

God, yes. "That's what I'm counting on."

"I'm repeating what is already obvious now. The desperate commit suicide because they see no other way out. She was backed into a corner."

He would never state the obvious unless he thought I was too dense to see it. "Yes. I want to find out who backed her into it."

"Treat it like murder."

I would. My brother would have agreed. "I will." It seemed a viable option, a cleansing move.

"In fact, I was using a similar theme in the Poe novel." By that he meant he had found something out about me while studying my family's history. I didn't like him rummaging through micro-fiche, reading the old clippings. He sighed and said, "Now I'll have to change it."

Rewriting. Reviewing. Chasing. We would always be in motion.

***

North Shore cats crooned in the night like hungry babies, leaping off garbage cans in the alley, sneaking past doorways and wrestling fish bones from one another in back of the club. A turquoise neon nimbus blazed down across the sidewalk, burning into darkness and flashing off the jewelry of ladies lined before the railings, waiting their turn to enter The Bridge.

Pasted on the door was a poster: dour black-and-white photograph of a sad-eyed Zenith Brite singing amidst shadow,

head thrown back, ringlets of hair draped across one cheek to
the corner of her mouth, thin trails of cigarette smoke weaving beyond her like incense before an altar, her hands touching the mike stand in a skilled display of erotica, nails short
but sharp, lips neither dry nor wet. The photo worked: substance and effect. You wanted to meet her. You were willing to
hear her sing.

The line was longer now than when I'd gotten on it at
nine o'clock. It was 10:20 and I knew that Zenith Brite would
be well into her second set. I was fifth from the door and my
patience, surprisingly, hadn't begun to wane yet.

Zenith Brite and her band were booked throughout October at The Bridge. She hadn't been a torch singer the last time
I'd seen her perform, but she had not been a headliner, either.
I'd never been to the club, but had heard it was the happening
spot to be if you liked torch singers, film-noir ambiance, lobster tail, and two-hundred-dollar-a-bottle champagne. From the
outside The Bridge looked like most clubs—large and attractive with the neon wash. In the daylight you could see the
boats setting out across Long Island Sound for Connecticut;
now you could glimpse a few running lights.

The bustle of cocktail waitresses and bartenders was the
only noise escaping the front door, blanketing any music Zenith Brite might be playing. For the past hour and a half I'd
watched the bouncers at the entrance turn away five teenagers,
escort four drunken men and their dates across the parking
lot, flirt with a dozen women by comparing them to sex-
goddess movie stars, and flex their muscles several thousand
times. They were dressed identically in red bow-ties, cummer-
bunds, black vests and sleeveless jackets so their cannon ball-
sized biceps bulged without restriction.

At twenty to eleven I was at the front of the line. A bouncer asked, "How are you doing tonight, sir?"

"Fine, thanks."

"Welcome to The Bridge. Enjoy the show."

I was escorted inside by a woman in net stockings who smiled warmly at me. "Will you be meeting friends or would you like to have a seat at the bar?"

"Neither," I said. "I'd appreciate a table for two as near to the stage as possible." I slipped her a fifty dollar bill. I wasn't sure it would go over well enough.

She smiled again, less warmly, and brought me to a small table slightly to one side of the stage, recessed in the shadows, directly in front of the piano. She left and the cocktail waitress came over. I ordered a beer.

Having gone without sleep for the last forty-eight hours, I was lulled by the milieu, though my back itched horribly. Non-sequitur thoughts formed a pastiche of somber connotations: Susan's taste resided deep in my mouth. When the beer came I sipped it slowly, looking around the room, watching the patrons drinking and talking. A clatter of drums brought my attention to the stage, where three musicians moved to their instruments. The guitarist and bassist ran through a number of quick scales while the drummer tapped away.

Zenith Brite appeared at the back of the room, dressed in a crimson silk chemise and skirt. She walked forward with a subtle look of determination etched into the set of her jaw, the same sad, attractive eyes as her poster. They were not as blue as Linda's, or as black as Susan's or mine. She seemed to hardly notice the audience she twined through, utterly focused on weaving her way to the stage. A lone spotlight followed her path and remained on her for the rest of the show.

Without any of the customary chatter, she sat at the piano and gently played at the high end of the keys, soft voice
beginning softly in those nether-regions where you're hearing
something beautiful but not fully aware of it yet. She hummed
the tune at first, staring at a patch of wall behind me. When
I noticed she was actually singing, it was as if the words were
suddenly *there*, her voice immediately strong and flaring, filling out the club the way lips fill out a kiss.

Her hair uncurled over her face, duplicating the photo
shot on the poster. Nice touch. She took no bows after any
song; instead, the music glided along, one piece moving into
the next. People felt compelled to clap anyway. The first few
seconds of each new number were drowned out by applause.
But the audience eventually caught on, realizing they were
breaking into the fluidity of her performance, and most of
them stopped. Couples stood and moved onto the dance floor.
A few hawkers cheered and pounded the table tops. The rest
of us listened, silent and entranced.

When she finished, the crowd erupted what it had been
holding back. The noise didn't appear to affect her. She smiled
demurely and gave a half-curtsy/half-bow, a short waving flick
of the wrist. She gestured for the band to stand beside her,
which they did, and then they stepped off to the sides as the
applause rose for her again. The spotlight went out as she
walked past me towards the bar. A CD player came to life, the
music canned and fuzzy.

Fans followed and gathered around her as she took a seat
at the bar. I didn't feel like pressing through the pack, so I did
my best to make eye contact with her without appearing to be
too demented. Ten minutes later she was politely listening to
one of the guys talk when she leaned forward and glanced my

way. Looking past me at the stage, she eventually focused on my face. Contact. She squinted and smiled, trying to place me; her eyes opened wide and some of the sadness solidified, mixed with perhaps a little apprehension. I loved the look. I grinned in a hopeless attempt to put her at ease. I raised my beer and gestured to the empty chair beside me. She excused herself from the gang and came over.

"Hi," she said. "I'm glad you made it to the show."

"I wouldn't have missed it," I said. Corny, but it was an establishing first line.

"You are ... Nat, right? Nate?"

"Nathaniel, yes." She sat and crossed her hands on the table-cloth. "There was a swarm of guys around you, but I didn't see the bartender bring you anything. Can I get you a drink?"

She tilted her head back, then forth, until she made up her mind. "Okay. Sure. A Diet Coke, please."

I flagged down a waitress and ordered another beer and a Diet Coke. The dull pulse of a headache was beginning.

I told Zenith Brite, "I've seen you perform at Sin City and Waves On The Bay, but ..."

"But the act is different now," she finished. Of course, rewrite, keep in motion. "When I first started as a singer I got hooked up with a guitarist and fronted this band called Nocturne. Original songs, but they were entirely his. The music was good, but he wouldn't let anyone get a single improvised lick in, no solos he hadn't explicitly wanted. That kind of rigidity became unbearable. I quit eight months ago and the others moved out to L.A., where they recently signed their first record deal." She frowned. "Should it even be called a *record deal*? They don't even make vinyl anymore. Anyhow, I stayed here on the Island, working with a new combo to get the sound I've always wanted." She smiled. "Does everything I just said sound too much like bio liner notes?"

She had an open, friendly manner. "Not at all. I was interested in the reason for your switch in styles. I'm glad you're doing what you want to be doing."

"As an author you're in a better position to understand that than most people."

"Maybe."

The pause lengthened. We knew we had gotten to the point where we were talking around the subject of Susan's death. The headache got worse, and so did the itching on my back. Our drinks came. She didn't know how to approach the topic, and though I'd been thinking about it the entire time I was standing on line out front, neither did I. I understood the sincerity in her silence, but we would get past it. I had my blood to take back.

Zenith beat me on the draw. Staring into her glass of soda she asked, "Were you a good friend of Susan's?"

"No, I hardly knew her. You?"

"Not at all," she said. "I only said hello to her in passing and wished her a happy birthday. Those were the only words we exchanged." Zenith moved her empty glass aside and sat back, puzzled. "She actually brought a lot of people around to meet me, sort of advertising me—but in a nice way. I didn't understand her doing that, but I didn't mind, either. Word of mouth is some of the best publicity you can get, especially in the Hamptons." She shook her head. "No, I didn't know Susan. I was invited to her party by a friend of a friend. Of a friend, perhaps."

I wondered if Susan had had any real friends at all, or if everyone in her life had simply been adrift in that same realm of passing acquaintances, each of us phantoms revolving around her. "Who?"

"Who invited me?"

"Yes."

She pointed vaguely across the room. "Richie. He walked in the door about two minutes ago while we were talking."

I followed her careless wave; it took me a minute to home in on who she was gesturing towards. People were chatting, laughing, hunched over their drinks, but it wasn't long before the shine of his teeth and ruby tie-pin brought my attention up short. His hair was wet and slicked back in a tight bun like he'd just leaped from the shower, and he was freshly shaved as midnight owls are bound to be. His boys surrounded him, fixed in their orbits. I watched as a waitress brought the peddler a carafe of wine.

"What's his name?"

Zenith gave me a confused grimace. "He's Richie Sutter." The look on her face made me suspect I had somehow put my foot in my mouth.

"Let me guess. He owns the club."

"Close enough. His father owns it. Richie just works the business." She dismissed him in the next instant and said, "It sounds strange, but I feel as though I'm doing something wrong tonight—just doing my show, sitting here—as if I'm not abiding by the rules. She just died yesterday." Her hair tumbled over her cheek again and she brushed it back.

"No rules," I said. "I'd like to meet him."

"Richie? Why?"

It was a good question. I wasn't prepared for good questions. There are times when you cannot work around the core of whatever it is you're feeling or thinking at the moment—

when white lies and tap-dancing evasions are less useful than cutting to the heart of the matter. "He passed a bag of coke to Susan last night."

She didn't say anything, but the lift of her eyebrows implied *So what?* then she looked down. "You sound as if you've got a vendetta."

"I'm not sure what I've got, Zenith."

"Looking for material for a book?"

"No."

The etchings of fear danced across her face again. "You're not thinking of causing trouble, are you?" She shot a glance over at him. I got the feeling she was trying to do me a considerable favor. "You wouldn't want to make trouble for him, Nathaniel."

"*Moi?*"

An older couple walked by and took the opportunity to stop at our table and commend Zenith's performance. Taking no notice of me, the lady and gentleman complimented her, saying the things I realized I should've said when she first sat down. *Death is everywhere.* It was. I'd been preoccupied.

The couple left and Zenith turned to face me, regarding me calmly. "Richie Sutter is wealthy, handsome, charming, and does pretty much whatever the hell he wants. Nocturne was into smack for a while and got connected in with Richie. That was a couple of years ago, before Richie's father fronted him the club. When the guitarist cut out I kept on working the gigs, playing my own music, working for the break. When The Bridge opened, Richie asked me to headline, and here I am." Her eyebrows tightened. "Nathaniel, I really don't know why I'm telling you all this, except that maybe you're a nice guy."

"I am," I said. I could barely keep from scratching the raw itch of Susan's scratches.

"I can see by that steely squint of yours that you want to ask if I'm his lover." I didn't. "The answer, which happens to be none of your business, is yes, no, and maybe. I didn't screw to get this job and I wouldn't screw to keep it. If you think drugs are what drove Susan Hartford to kill herself, then, well, I couldn't argue with you because I didn't know her. But even if they were, that would be her fault, wouldn't it?"

"Maybe," I said.

With the air of argument, Zenith was about to say something else but didn't get the chance. A large man with a size forty-six neck stepped over to us, hands clenched at his waist. He bent over the table and said to her, "Mr. Sutter asked that you and your friend please join him at his private table, Miss Brite."

She looked at me and I smiled my most appealing smile. No ladies in the club swooned or passed out at my feet.

"Um," Zenith said.

"Of course," I said.

Her eyes widened and the impatient sigh she gave me must've been audible across the room. As she stood, I could tell she felt she had somehow played into my hand, and that the trouble she had warned me off of was most definitely ensuing.

Zenith walked over and took Richie Sutter's hand the way children step up to strangers who are holding candy and ice cream out. He did not stand up to meet her, but motioned to the seats beside him. I didn't know why he had bouncers around the club as well as an entourage of grim-faced, stone-jawed men. He was either paranoid or not well liked.

"Zenith, you were sensational as always," he told her. "I'm sorry I missed the third set, but I've been hearing nothing but praise for your performance."

"Thank you, Richie."

"How did the two new songs go? Did you manage to iron out the reprisal?"

"Yes," she said. "I think we're going to start adding them to the play sheet."

He turned to me. "Pardon my manners. I'm Richie Sutter. Please have a seat."

"Richie," Zenith said. "This is Nathaniel Follows."

I wouldn't have thought it possible, but the peddler's smile grew even larger when he got hold of my name; it did not warm the proverbial cockles of my heart. It was like being in the front row of *Jaws*, like looking at my brother. Knowing someone's name takes away any power they might find in the shadows of anonymity. "Pleased to meet you, Nathaniel."

I shook his hand.

Richie Sutter was one of those rare men who have a broad realm of expression without having to alter their facial muscles very much. Half a twist of his upper lip could make the difference between a grin, a leer, and a wince. His manner was founded on an economy of humanity. Most people fill up their personal space, either brightening it or darkening it, but always existing within it. Richie Sutter was an exception who drew himself up inside his own aura, cleverly hiding in the open. Sitting next to him, I could feel the pull like the current of a whirlpool. He rarely closed his mouth, usually leaving his sparkling teeth on view. His eyes were polished black gems.

I was determined not to bring up Susan first. Yesterday, as I'd stumbled through the crowd while the cops sifted through, I hadn't noticed Richie or Zenith among those remaining and concluded they took off before the police arrived.

"I seem to recall seeing you at the Hartford Party last night," he said. "Or am I mistaken?"

"I was Susan's date, in a manner of speaking."

"Oh really? I wasn't aware of that. I didn't think she had a steady."

"If she did, I wasn't it. Last night was my first time ever inside a house on Dune Road." I looked around the room, hearing laughter and slow music playing from the jukebox, "In fact, I don't frequent clubs much anymore, and I don't think I've ever been in one quite like this. Between Zenith's haunting ballads, the champagne, a nice cool atmosphere, and the waitresses' stockings and mini-skirts, I'd say you have the right amount of class to bring customers in and hold onto them. Did Susan come here often?"

He moistened his lips. "A tragedy," he mused.

"Yes," I agreed.

"She was a darling girl, but ..." He let the *but* hang in the air like a dangling noose, guiding it with a wave of his hand. "But I can't say the taking of her own life surprised me greatly."

His manner began to grate. He was so slick I started feeling greasy just sitting at the same table. You could feel him enveloping the area around himself. I had a gut notion that if I threw a book of matches at him it would vanish rather than touch him. I smiled and kept a level, friendly tone. "Now why would you say that a wealthy, beautiful nineteen-year-old girl committing suicide on her birthday doesn't shock the absolute hell out of you, Richie?"

One of his boys had a spiked hairdo that made him look like the Statue of Liberty; the dude uncrossed his arms and glared at me, but the Peddler's teeth kept right on gleaming. I really did like him a lot, in a fathomless way.

"Some people are destined to be victims, I believe," Richie Sutter said. "Whether they are born with that mentality or if it grows within them over their lives, I don't know. They bemoan their fate and curse their lives and complain about misfortune, yet do nothing to change their circumstances. They refuse to even make an effort. Whining is easier than struggling. It is better to pout than it is to fight. Or work. Or commit to a project. Or take a chance. They often choose to prostitute themselves in one way or another, maybe sexually, maybe spiritually, enslaving themselves until they've sold all they are and virtually nothing remains."

Zenith said, "Perhaps they are simply too scared."

He looked mildly astonished that she had spoken. "Fear is the murderer of soul. Desperation is an end rather than a means. It is my belief that death is the end of life, whereas apathy is its antithesis." I liked that line and vowed to steal it. He sipped his wine. "What a waste." He said it as though he'd just found a dent in the fender of his car. "I wonder if she was aware of all the heartache she'd leave behind."

"I wondered about that, too," I said.

"Yes?"

"And something else," I said.

"Hm. What about?" he asked.

"Whether she took all your coke with her out the window. Now that really would've been a terrible waste, wouldn't it, Richie?"

It was a weak goad, but it worked. For an instant his smile faltered, but you had to have been watching closely to catch it. Liberty made a noise and took a step forward; it was a tactic that was supposed to make me cringe. I eyed the peddler's silverware, the knife crossed over the fork. I shifted in my seat; I was good with my left hand and could grab it easily. I wondered what I should cut first.

I faced his spiked doo, and said, "Didn't your mother ever tell you that steroids shrivel your gonads?"

Liberty fumed but quit coming at me. Zenith groaned.

The peddler showed me his sharp white teeth some more. "It's getting rather late and I have some business to attend to," he said. "Goodnight, Mr. Follows. It was rather entertaining speaking with you."

Zenith slipped out beside me, took my elbow, and quickly walked me to the front door. "Smart," she said. "Very smart. Are you naturally this aggressive or do you just enjoy full body casts?"

"You're not implying that your pal Richie would administer harm upon my well-being, are you?"

Outside, it was drizzling. I leaned against my Mustang, breathing in the cool fresh air. The wind had risen, keening eerily as the tops of trees swayed, brown and red leaves whirling across the parking lot, jammed into sewer grates. The rain roared down against my migraine, spilling over rooftops, spraying thickly off the Long Island Sound. I stood in it for a minute, feeling the surge of vitality that icy water on your face can bring. Hazy moonlight soaked through the clouds, and for a second I thought I glimpsed a moonbow.

The back of my neck crawled as if the eyes of the dead children were upon me.

5

Shrieking high winds and pounding rain kept me awake. The
elms lining my building scraped against the windows, and
Achilles gave a yelp whenever an especially loud *thwack* resounded. Finally, fatigue caught up with me, and the weight
of events over the past three days crashed down like a toppled
wall, and I tumbled into dreamless sleep.

I was out cold for thirteen hours and woke up with a
heaviness of mind and muscle that took a five mile run in the
rain to work off.

My back bled.

When I got home, Carrie was sitting on my doorstep slapping my mail and newspaper against her leg; her hair was
damp and limp and tussled in every direction, frizzing at the
ends the way it does on soggy days like this. Her breath made
small explosions of steam in the air, and she seemed to be so
bored she could no longer see straight. I was brought up short
finding her here, waiting for me like a soothsayer, knowing
she was Linda's best friend.

Carrie had been going out with Jack off and on since we

were in high school, but I never considered her a friend of mine until a year ago. Last Christmas she and Jack invited me to dinner, and ten minutes after I arrived Jack received word that his partner had been winged after stumbling into a holdup. With a grim smile Jack handed me a present, said "Merry Christmas," and left, his utter calm unaltered.

And so, it happened: Carrie and I somehow got entwined in conversation and spent most of the night on a corner of the couch making out. At one point she started crying, admitting how scared she would be to marry a cop; less than an hour later she cursed a mean streak, wondering if the bastard would *ever* ask her to marry him. We drank too much and made it to the bed, and at midnight, while we laid there atop each other, she forced me to open my present; it was the book on the fifteen most efficient ways to kill someone.

"Ooh, Christ, you stink as badly as boiled cabbage," she said.

"And a fine good morning to you, too."

I unlocked my door and the dogs darted out at her—twitching backsides, wagging tails, lolling tongues—the sum of their parts greater than the whole, swarming over her like a pack of rats. Carrie owned four sycophant cats, and for someone who had just insulted my odor it was apparent she had no qualms with her own Tender Vittles perfume. Achilles went into a sneezing fit.

"Get these beasts off me!"

I yanked the dogs away, but they refused to go far, hovering about her for a time before laying down at her feet, sniffing joyously.

"Have a seat," I told her, ducking into the bathroom to get towels for both of us. I said, "How long were you waiting for me?"

"Not too long. Less than half an hour, I guess. I figured we could go out to Bennigan's for lunch."

"Sounds good."

She tossed the mail and paper on the couch and began drying her hair with that special massaging action some girls have, flipping her long curls back and forth from underneath. "But not until you take a shower."

"Take one with me," I said.

She laughed and snapped the towel at me. I tried to smile and failed. She didn't notice.

I sat at my weight bench; the muscles in my legs tight and powerful while my upper chest and arms still felt sluggish and knotted. "I have to work out for another thirty minutes or I'll tighten up into Quasimodo."

"Is it true that Lon Chaney wore a harness in *The Hunchback of Notre Dame* that was torturous after only fifteen or twenty minutes?"

"No," I said.

She shrugged. "Too bad."

I laid down on the bench, slid under the bar, careful of my back, and started doing presses with two-twenty.

"Since when are you up for the Arnie Schwartzeneggar fitness award?"

"Just doing my part to keep America healthy."

She made a noise like "harumph," stepped daintily around the dogs, and fell back on the couch.

She said, "You've got a few self-addressed stamped envelopes here."

"Happens every day," I breathed out. "Rejections."

"Editors returning your stuff? You must spend more on postage having your stories returned to you than you could ever make selling them."

"You're right," I said.

"I don't see why you don't teach creative writing on the side to bring in some extra money. You only write for a couple of hours a day and the rest of the time you're just sitting around."

"The rest of the day I'm sitting around thinking of things to write."

"It's still only sitting around."

"Maybe. But it's what I do."

"Humph," she went.

I grit my teeth, shoving the bar up for the tenth time, then relaxing before I started my second rep. "Are you in this happy state of mind for any particular reason?"

Again came the "humph" noise, a short blast of air that, if it had been longer and we'd been beneath a full moon, might have passed for a forlorn sigh.

She said, "About Linda ..."

"I really don't want to talk about it."

"Yes, you do. I can tell."

"No," I said. "I don't."

"Denial won't make you feel better."

I slid back under the weights and began a second set of presses. "I'm not denying anything. I just don't want to talk about it."

"You'll feel much better if you tell me what happened, Nathaniel."

"Now why would you think that, Carrie?"

She brought her heels back against the legs of the couch with enough force to jolt Ulysses off the floor. She'd done the same at Christmas, finally kicking her legs down after we were through, snapping her feet down beside me, turning over in my arms. "Because that's what you're supposed to do! You're supposed to come to me and tell your side of things—you yell and bitch and ask a million questions. 'What did she say, what did she admit to you? Is there any chance she'll take me back again?' And because I promised her not to tell you anything I have to put up a stone facade which you eventually break through by sheer persistence and force me to give you the details of all that emotional stuff that you *are* denying. I'm the middle ground where you two get to exchange your feelings without having to face one another."

"Not quite," I said.

While I concentrated on steady breathing and control, Carrie got up and wandered around my living room. With peripheral vision I watched as she went to the bookcase and took novels down, wearily flipping through pages, replacing the books. I finished my second set but was too impatient to wait before I began the third. I had a hard time imagining how much effort guys like Liberty put into their daily workouts as I hefted the bar again.

She turned while I grunted. She was here for a reason I couldn't put a finger on: Linda had already given her the scoop of our break-up, yet I didn't believe that in itself could get Carrie upset. She wasn't seeking my version of the split, especially since I'd made no attempts to bend her ear or cry on her shoulder. No. She didn't care, I didn't care, Linda didn't care.

Carrie humphed again. She was more tentative than usual, and her sulky mood gave me cause to believe she wanted to talk about her and Jack. I didn't want to hear it.

Her perusal brought her to my desk, an area filled with piles of deep-sixed chapters and first-version manuscripts that had miscarried or died in labor: they were the bits and pieces

I'd cannibalize for the next Jacob Browning novel, if I ever went back to it. She ran her fingers over the keypad of my computer. The weights were getting heavier by the second, but it felt good to keep going. Veins bulged along my forearms, pulse rising, and I started gasping for breath, pushing my limit, then snorting, finally feeling it in my balls, and I hooked into something deep.

"Jesus, what's gotten into you?" Carrie said. "Something sure as hell has you fired up." She spun and picked up my notebook, glancing through it while making small "hm" sounds of interest. Her ass wiggled. She shut my notebook closed with finality. The light in her eyes said, "shit," about five seconds before she did.

"Shit, that address on the cover," she said, staring at me. "Dune Road. I've seen that before. Today." She stepped over to the couch, grabbed the paper and snapped it open. "There's only a small follow-up story today, but it was yesterday's headlines. About some rich kid committing suicide, right? What are you doing? Background for another novel?"

"No," I said.

I didn't want to tell her anything; I didn't want to keep giving out information like Halloween candy—here's one for you, and you, and one for you, too. Before heading off to The Bridge last night, I'd read the newspaper articles recounting what had gone on at the party. The basic facts were correct; no reporters had gathered anything else from the police or EMTs or gatherers at the scene. I'd spent most of the afternoon and early evening in the library, researching everything I could about Susan's family.

Lowell Hartford was an entrepreneur who made his money hand over fist in any number of enterprises. He dealt in computers, antiques, and the international exchange of cultural icons and treasures for various museums. I thought it strange that his home did not reflect his interest in fine arts. He was a corporate president and world traveler, but he didn't come from old wealth—there had been long retrospectives in the business sections showing how he'd risen from the slums of Chicago. I'd gone back five years in the microfiche and come up with everything I could on Hartford and his family. There were short pieces in the society pages when both Jordan and Susan had their debutante balls at sixteen. Other articles reported the active involvement of their mother, Sarah, in efforts to find low-cost housing for the homeless, participation in drug-awareness campaigns, and a strong stance against pornography and animal experimentation.

In reverse-video on the microfiche, where the photographs used in the papers appear in negative, I couldn't truly make out what kind of an image Lowell Hartford presented. But I saw he didn't smile much.

"Are you listening to me?" Carrie asked, softly.

"Yes," I said.

"Do you want to, uh, mess around?" she asked, tentatively, unsure of herself in my life, but not of herself.

"Yes," I said.

I packed on more weights, doing flys now to work the pecs and lats, the sweat feeling good, contours of my arms and chest tightening and becoming more defined. Straining, I kept a quick pace, arms wide open and then closing, the metal weights clanging as I brought them together over me, then eased them back down to the floor, then up again. Ulysses' head bobbed back and forth as he watched me.

"You're making me hot," she said "sweating like that. Makes me think of our past Yuletide offerings."

I laughed and finished my workout. I stood and went to her; she *was* hot, her hands casually passing over her blouse, grazing her breasts, her throat reddening.

Maybe the fact that Jack still hadn't proposed was starting to make her shaky again; after ten years it was understandable. At twenty-seven she swore her biological clock was winding down; her maternal instincts came to the forefront whenever she attended baby showers. She used to babysit for Randy in order to allow Linda and me a night out for ourselves, back when we'd wanted that night. I didn't care much for reasons now, just what we were about to do.

***

Later, when she awoke, I pretended to be asleep; she dressed and left in silence, knowing I was faking. I took a shower and tried do some work on the book, but the words wouldn't come. The blinking green cursor sat in the upper corner of my computer screen, winking and waiting for me to pull the narrative from my mind. It wasn't there anymore. I was barely able to remember the plot I'd held so clearly on the Point, the one which had been coming so quick and easily two days ago. A substantial amount of my life seemed to have passed in only a handful of hours. It felt as if this first week of October would fill more than half my biography.

Tenacity is a character trait both admired and despised. As I watched the cursor blink, I felt the vice-grips of obsession tightening at my temples. My brother used to take painkillers by the dozens, emptying bottles in his mouth, none of the medication helping; he'd lost his faith in the doctors early on. The nerves in my fingers danced, and with some amazement I realized that for a man who prided himself on his idleness,

I was actually craving action. It was dangerous for a Follows to feel that way. Inertia was beginning to unravel control. Tricks were being played. The walls were folding and unfolding. I saw Susan falling, each frame unwinding as perfectly as the last, every film ending with the same splash of red. I dug the heels of my hands into my eyes.

Thank Christ the phone rang.

The voice on the other end said, "Nathaniel," with such vehemence that for a second I didn't realize it was my own name. She'd been crying for a long time and wasn't nearly finished, and the hitches in her breath crackled over the line, breaking my name into seven syllables. "Nathaniel."

"Jordan?"

She tried to say more, but whatever it was became trapped in a long, winding sob. The rain was coming down harder, slashing at the glass panes, the walls rumbling from the wind. I had trouble hearing.

"Calm down, Jordan. You're going to hyperventilate. Force yourself to take deep breaths."

The crying went on while I waited in silence, trying to find something to say and knowing there was nothing. I could hear the saliva thickening in her mouth, choking her; she coughed and gagged and wept. Maybe three minutes passed before she could speak again, and then only in a hoarse whisper.

"I'm sorry, Nathaniel," she said. "I don't know why I even decided to call you, but I needed to talk and I couldn't think of anyone else who would bother to listen."

"I'll listen," I said.

"My parents should be returning from Cairo sometime tomorrow. I don't think they know what's happened. I tried several times over the past two days to get them at their hotel, but the goddamn Middle Eastern operator couldn't put me through. I was informed that the police got in touch with the manager, but somehow he got the story screwed up. I think my parents believe Susan's been arrested."

"Arrested?"

"A telegram came about an hour ago. It said: 'Call Meachum and explain everything. Home as soon as possible.' Francis Meachum is our lawyer. Why would my parents want me to call the lawyer unless they thought my sister was in jail? What am I going to tell them?" she growled, the hysteria having changed into fury now. "I'm the big sister. They told me to look after her."

"It wasn't your fault, Jordan."

"My father won't think that. You don't know him. He will blame me."

She sounded convinced. Static filled the line for a few seconds, the rain rattling the windows like tricksters on Halloween. The dogs were running in circles, the dead leaf smell of the storm working into the room. Branches threatened to shatter the glass. "He'll be wrong."

"Thanks for saying it, but no matter how old I get I'll always be his little girl, and I'll always act it. And that is my fault. I'm afraid of him, and I can't explain why. He's never so much as raised his voice. Not really." She bit down a whimper. "And I can't even think about what my Mom will go through when she finds out the truth."

"Did they call Susan for her birthday?"

"I'm not sure. As you know, I was fairly wrecked at the party, and if they did phone I missed it. They sent her an Egyptian amulet my father bought in Alexandria. It came a day early by special delivery." Her manner turned soft again, and I could hear the tremolo of her fear. "You were with her, Nathaniel. You know what happened."

"No," I said. "I don't."

She ignored me. "I got your number off her nightstand, where she had it stuck under the phone. Will you come tomorrow? Will you tell them? There's no reason for you to agree, but will you?"

"Yes," I said.

Lowell Hartford struck me as a man who would abhor failure, and Susan had been a girl filled with such deep self-deprecation it had bled through. I had been there. And in my own fashion I, too, was afraid to face Susan's parents. I had played my part as the rapist to the hilt, the capper of self-destruction—she wanted to be fucked hard, and I'd wanted to kill her with little deaths, with large deaths, but how would it have been if only I'd spoken other words and shown the slightest tenderness? The blood taste filled my mouth the way my blood had filled Susan's.

"Yes," I repeated.

"Thank you."

And, as if the entire conversation had been merely gauze swathing a single cut, I said in a rush of words, "How did Susan get those scars all over her body?"

Jordan said, "What scars?"

***

The temperature continued to drop throughout the night, and by eleven AM an early winter freeze was in effect. I wore a charcoal suit and gray shirt and tie for my second visit to the Hartford home. The now freezing rain fell heavily, and in a house with as many windows as this one had—the smears of ice were thick on every pane—I was struck with a slight sense of claustrophobia, as if I were in a submarine. Without the party, the mansion squatted gloomy and forlorn. The waves smashed the shore, and the sound traveled well.

Like a magnet, the patio doors constantly drew my attention back to them, but there was nothing to see. Even through the blur of the downfall I could tell the patio furniture had been removed.

Jordan met my glance. She was more than scared, she was terrified, and I thought I could understand why. On my bureau I have a photograph from circa nineteen thirty which shows my grandmother staring into the camera with a very self-conscious smile—most of her teeth were gone by then—her skirt flanked by my mother and aunt, who were perhaps six and five. Grandma is short, but neither stocky nor frail, with a gleam that speaks volumes of hardships but accedes no remorse. She is slightly stooped from bending over her sewing machine for sixteen hours a day, and her arms are strong enough to lug blocks of ice four stories from the street to the ice box. My mother and aunt are already beginning to get that edge about them, in the contours of their meager grins, which warned they would become women who could toil, bear children, run a household and survive, yet never learn to cook well because they discovered early to eat whatever was put on the plate before them.

Lowell Hartford had very much the same look about himself, as though he had played every poor hand dealt him and turned it to his advantage. He was only five-five and one hundred fifty pounds, clean-shaven but with the hint of a heavy blue-black beard, eyebrows peaking in that Mike Tyson/ Jack Nicholson satanic arch.

Even with his eyes shut, sitting in his leather chair in the den, he still glared, his face recently weathered by the Egyptian sun. His wife Sarah sat in the divan beside Jordan, one arm around her daughter, nervously patting her shoulder. Nobody cried and nobody went out of their way to comfort anyone else. Nobody was talking either. Mrs. Hartford looked as though she'd swallowed three times her normal dosage of valium.

On yet another settee, across from Hartford himself, I sat with Francis Meachum, the lawyer and family friend who held a glass of scotch and water tightly enough to whiten his incredibly hairy knuckles. He kept looking at me levelly, steadfast, and I knew he recognized my name. The lawyer who'd gotten my father off was famous among his brethren; he'd shown the world just what loopholes could do. Like Richie Sutter, the fact that Meachum knew my name gave him some power over me.

"It makes no sense," Sarah Hartford said, pat, pat, patting away, her pale hand flapping up and down on Jordan's shoulder like the wing of a pigeon. Sorrow was tactile around us, filling the room. "I can't understand. It makes no sense. No sense at all. She had everything. What could have happened?" Without pausing for breath she went on. "Would anyone like coffee? Or a drink? A sandwich? You must be hungry, Lowell. Such dreadful food on the plane for first class, you hardly ate a thing."

"It'll be okay, Mom," Jordan said.

Francis Meachum was a rotund fellow with a terrible toupee and nostril hairs longer than your average garden snake. He had one of those strangely modulating voices that scattered cadences. His smile was too broad, and he stared down at himself almost as much as he stared at me, picking lint off his

jacket, playing with his watch band, and smoothing his pant
legs every few minutes, always touching himself. He was a prime
candidate to join the Fat Ernies. I also couldn't get over the
smell of his aftershave, a strange and almost feminine scent.

Meachum licked his wide lips, and gave Mrs. Hartford a
patronizing smile, which she returned. "No one could suspect, Sarah," he said. "I visited frequently while you were out
of the States, and yet no one could have guessed our Susan
would be dreaming of taking her own life."

Sarah Hartfod's hand flapped faster. "But if we were *here*
... then ..."

"Nothing would have been changed," Meachum said, his
voice hardening, the sing-song ending. "Her motivations were
entirely her own. Purely. Ever since she was a child she was a
willful and stubborn girl, listening to no one but herself, ac-
cepting no advice, and as argumentative as the year is long. If
Susan wasn't being reprimanded in school, then she was running away. How many times were we taken into court on
juvenile delinquency charges?"

"At least a dozen."

"More than a dozen. She was a young woman who lived
her own life, and no matter how you might have tried you
would not have been able to alter events. Suicide is the most
selfish form of expression."

A lot of people would have agreed with him, but he was
wrong—more off-base than he could ever know—and I didn't
like his self-righteous tone. "Your sensitivity is going to have
me blubbering all over the place, Mr. Meachum."

"What?" he said, puzzled. After a half a minute, as if at
least hearing me, he repeated much louder, "What?" Irate, throwing a how-dare-you attitude. "What?" I wondered how Susan

would have liked listening to that on a day to day basis. He gazed at me and curled his lip, the nose hairs slithering. He would tell Hartford all about my brother and father as soon as I left, but he wouldn't say anything now. He went back to staring, like he was watching some strange and macabre film unwinding in his mind—the way D.B. used to look at the dogs.

"Where is the body?" Hartford broke in, without opening his eyes.

At the word "body," Mrs. Hartford's hand beat faster. It caught Jordan all wrong, too, and she sank lower in her seat.

"White's Funeral Home," Francis Meachum replied. There was an ugly tone in his voice, as if he hated White, or funeral homes. "The arrangements have already been made. The funeral will be held tomorrow."

Jordan nodded. I noticed she no longer used make-up to alter her natural features quite so much. Although her hair was still California-blond, she had tamed the wildness from it so the curls framed her heart-shaped face. She seemed so much like her sister I almost couldn't stand looking at her. "The police want to talk with you, Dad. They said to call the minute you got back."

"That can wait." With the intensity of Lazarus awakening from the pit, Lowell Hartford's eyes snapped open. I felt a twinge; none of the newspaper accounts had properly described the kind of energy he radiated. With his fist tucked under his chin, he glanced at each of us for a moment, resting his gaze on his daughter, then shifting it over to me.

He was a man who believed in angles, and he figured I must have one. Perhaps he thought I would somehow try to extort money from him, or get a free ride by sweeping Jordan off her feet, having failed with Susan. Maybe he had listened to Fatter Ernie and was preparing his revenge upon me. I could feel the push of his glare, probing my nature. Our staring match lasted only a handful of seconds, but the pressure was incredible. He felt it, too.

"What's your story, Follows?" he asked.

At length I repeated what I'd told Lieutenant Smithfield; I told him that Susan and I had slept together because I suspected that Jordan would eventually admit as much to her father; if she didn't offer up the fact willingly then, no doubt she'd be forced to do so by her respect for the power dwelling within his small, wiry frame.

Mrs. Hartford said, "My. My, my. Dear."

Meachum made a grandiose gesture with his scotch glass. "A promiscuous girl, as well," he said sadly. "That kind of behavior only proves my point."

"What point?" I asked.

His eyes narrowed and he took a long pull of his drink. I got the feeling he was putting on a show for Hartford, merely playing the judgmental type without the proper wrath, calling names like a child, histrionic without substance, in order to leave the Hartford family guiltless for what they themselves might be wanting to say. He was the mouthpiece for the dumb. He was prepared, and his role was well written, and I wondered what he was when he wasn't acting.

Jordan said, "But, Daddy ..."

If she had remained silent, the wall Hartford had erected around his heartbreak might not have cracked and poured out the poison building behind the dam. Or if it did, he might have directed its tide against me.

But by opening herself, she gave him a place to purge himself. The fire flared in his cheeks, and he virtually tossed himself out of his chair. "Jordan," he whispered. She threw back her shoulders, sitting bolt upright, her muscles locked in that position. "You never learned to appreciate anything. The finest schools, tutors, clothes, vacations across the world, anything you ever wanted and yet you sift through the filth, calling every undesirable and miscreant you trip over your goddamned friend! And for your own sister's birthday you invite them to our home! My home!"

He raised his hand and slapped her, an extremely light and glancing blow, hardly a slap at all, then brought his hand up again for emphasis. I slipped out of my seat and firmly gripped his wrist. He reminded me a little too much of my own father right then.

Hurting me.

He spun around. "Get away from me," he spat in my face. I had six inches and fifty pounds on him, and I struggled to keep a tight hold.

I said, "Touch her again and I will knock you through the fireplace, Mr. Hartford."

His jaw dropped.

"Lowell, for God's sake," Francis Meachum said, eyeing me, redirecting the game. He almost grinned. "You're filled with grief. Don't take it out on your one remaining daughter. Come sit down."

Hartford looked at his wife and saw the tears trailing down her cheeks, her nose running wildly without a sniffle, eyes glazed as she stared into space, hand still patting Jordan's shoulder. Her neck firmed like a goiter. He bent his head, his austere manner ruptured, perhaps, by shame.

"Yes," he murmured. "You're right, of course." I let go of his wrist and he moved towards Jordan and opened his arms.

She'd been waiting for some sign of forgiveness from her father, anything to take away her own mislaid guilt. She wrapped herself around him. Hartford hugged her tightly, cradling her, and then draped his other arm around his wife, so that the three of them swayed and rocked to the tune of sorrow. He stared at me over his daughter's shoulder and said, "Get out of my house, Follows."

I half-expected him to add *And never darken my doorstep again.*

Meachum smiled for the first time all night.

I cut out. The torrential rain smashed down on the Mustang. I'd learned more about Susan this morning, about her family and what it might have been like to live in such surroundings—I'd learned she might be more like me than I'd thought previously.

Driving up Dune Road with my wipers doing an ineffectual job of clearing my vision, I decided that I, too, wasn't doing enough.

I had to find out about her scars.

6

White's Funeral Home jutted from a backdrop of hill, an impressive piece of architecture of curious design that brought to mind antebellum Southern mansions: fat columns, porticos, and a sharply-pointed roof edged with intricate lattice work. The gnarled tree out front would have made the property seem less pretentious if only it had a rope swing with a couple of kids playing on a tire. According to the metal plaque screwed into the brick pillar at the base of the drive, the residence had been bought and sold by the Vanderbilts long before the conversion to its current status.

I walked up the slate steps, opened the door, and stepped inside a dimly-lit hallway paneled in mahogany. High, standing ashtrays, vases filled with fading flowers, and ceramic urns resting on pedestals lined the corridor. I was a day early for the viewing of Susan's body, but I thought if anyone could identify what made those scars, it would be the mortician. Why he might tell me, I didn't know yet. *Car accident* kept coming to mind, and something kept pushing it away.

The wide reception area opened into two reposing rooms:

Chapel A was occupied by the family and friends of
ARMANDO SANCHEZ, and Chapel B held a handful of
elderly stragglers for one MICHAEL TORRASSINO. The rooms
were filled with the formal draperies, mass cards, wreathes,
and rows of padded folding chairs.

Sanchez was either highly beloved or he owed money to a
lot of people; women and men were weeping unabashedly in
the room, shrieking and moaning, throwing themselves at
one another and calling on saints I'd never heard of. A girl sat
alone in the back row, a mixed look of confusion and sadness
wearing heavy on her pretty Latino features. My heart dropped
a notch as I moved farther down the corridor, crammed with
the dread of solemnity that places like churches and cemeter-
ies and other dwellings of the dead force upon us.

There is such a strong expectation for you to go through
the ritual of kneeling at the side of the casket, whispering
prayers your mouth cannot quite form the right words to,
that your mind, with all its religious instructions, can no
longer remember. If you cry you are ashamed, and if you
don't cry you are even more ashamed, and it is almost impossible to say a heartfelt goodbye to the pasty-faced, poorly-dressed,
disemboweled mannequin in the coffin, or make yourself believe it is the person you once loved.

Or once hated. For my father's funeral it snowed like the
start of a second ice age. A January morning only a few days
past New Year's, a time when families should be indoors drinking hot chocolate, playing Monopoly, and watching the tradi-
tional holiday movies. A season for children, when the after-
effects of Christmas haven't totally worn away and you haven't
managed to break all your new toys yet.

I was sixteen, no more a child. I hadn't been one for a

long time. Pine trees in the cemetery precariously held up tons of wet snow. The blizzard pelted us, like sinners being stoned, the skies heaving. Faces of friends, strangers, and enemies were lost in the swirling squall. The roses we threw into his grave lost their color to frost, glistening white ice shining. The priest's robes were great crystal wings beating like the vanguard of Gabriel. His words were squandered in the blizzard, but his voice was strong and appealing. Although the context could not be distinguished, his resolve was clear.

My father would have enjoyed the idea of snow spiraling down to escort him to Hell. He'd spent more time on my sled than I ever did. The standard fare of snowmen with corn cob pipes, button noses, and eyes made out of coal were beneath his wintry skill: we had warring snow-Godzillas and ice-triceratops facing each other across our back lawn, built over the ten-foot-deep graves. He opened the patio water pipe and used the hose to spray high into the trees, transforming the yard into a realm of mighty snowbeasts and gigantic icicles hanging from a glass forest.

"Are you all right, son?" someone asked, behind me.

Uh huh, yeah, it's good, it's so good.

I wheeled and saw a woman of about sixty, holding a lit cigarette, puffing madly. "I'm sorry, dear, I didn't mean to startle you." She wore a tight permanent and a black dress that showed she still had curves in the right places, and a few in the wrong places, too. "Funerals can give you creeps, isn't it the truth? Your color's back now. I just stepped outside for a cigarette. Do you think that's bad form? I couldn't care less what those cockroaches in his family think." She reached into her purse and pulled out a pack of Menthol 100s. "Would you like one?"

"No, thanks."

"Yes, well, you're young," she said, rather non-sequitur. She cocked her head. "You haven't seen much death, yet. But when you start to slide into your forties and fifties, almost all of your lifelong friends begin dropping like flies. This year alone I've lost my father, two sisters, and now my third husband. I could tell you stories."

Eager to talk, she raised her voice over the bleating of the Sanchezes in the other chapel. "Heart attacks, breast cancer, liver failure. My youngest sister, Rosie, died of a broken leg. Can you imagine? A broken leg. A bone splinter moved through her bloodstream right into her heart. I read a book once where that happened, but who believes such crazy things? It gets so you can't remember who's here, who's gone, and who's in the process of going. My mother is going, I think, but she doesn't want to hear. It gets so you expect to hear they're dead." She snaked her arm around mine and asked, "Are you here for my Mike?"

"No," I said.

"I thought maybe you were a neighbor's son, or a nephew I never met. He has seven or eight of them down in Florida somewhere. We were only married for twelve years." The tip of the cigarette flared as she took a long drag, moving awkwardly to the ashtray, as if both hips were broken. "He's the third I've buried. Three, can you imagine? And he wasn't but forty-seven. I'm starting to feel like a goddamn praying mantis."

"I'm sorry."

"Thank you, dear." The smoke poured from her mouth, lips waxy and too red, the curves curving more than they should have, as if flesh, and the skeleton beneath, were changing, moving beneath the mourning dress.

"Nice talking to you," she said.

"And you."

I passed another reposing room where various caskets sat on display with the price tags propped on tiny satin pillows. The twin doors to Chapel C and D were shut. I didn't try them. The layout of the house was awkward because the living rooms had been remodeled into parlors, and the back quarters had become the work areas. The director's room was down another short corridor, and loomed like the pricipal's office.

Finally, I came to an oak door with a sign that read MR. ARCHIBALD REMFREY: FUNERAL DIRECTOR. It sounded like the type of name that would have gotten him beaten up a lot on the playground. I knocked and waited. There was no answer. I tried again with the side of my fist, and this time the door was thrown open. He did, in fact, share a passing resemblance to my high school principal.

"Yes?"

Red tufts of hair shot from behind Remfrey's ears and a few rust-colored wisps dappled his head, otherwise he was entirely bald. His thin-lipped smile tattooed his face, making him appear clownish and moronic. That would help because my story was simple and stupid.

"How do you do, Mr. Remfrey. My name is Paul Prescott. I apologize for disturbing you."

"Not at all, not at all. How may I help you, sir?"

"I am ... I was Susan Hartford's fiancé."

Remfrey did a double-take. "Oh, my," he said, reaching out for a consoling touch on my elbow. "The young lady. I *am* sorry for your loss, Mr. Prescott."

I didn't think palming him a fifty was going to go over as well as it had with the cocktail waitress. I was counting on him believing that someone who was going to marry into the

Hartford family came from wealth and power himself. "Thank you. But I'm afraid I have a very sensitive request to ask."

"I assure you, sir," he said proudly, "that at White's Funeral Home we do our utmost to keep our patrons extremely happy."

I almost laughed. "I'm sure you do, Remfrey, and I'm glad for it." Lowell Hartford had taken to calling me by my surname to show his authority. I thought to follow his example on how to make people nervous. "You see, I've been called out of the States on urgent business, and would like to have an early, private viewing of her body."

His eyes strained to flee his skull. "Oh no," he said. "No, Mr. Prescott, I'm afraid that isn't possible. What you're asking is positively forbidden. We have strict regulations about that sort of thing."

"I understand, Remfrey, we wouldn't want just *anybody* wandering about a funeral home, but if you realized just how little time Susan and I had been able to spend together before ..."

"I'm sorry, sir, but it's absolutely out of the question." There was a heavy undertone of plaintiveness in his voice. "Quite."

There's something to be said for the pit-bull approach; I kept at him. "I've been called away to Marseilles on a delicate mission of national interest, and I won't be able to attend the services."

"Oh dear, it is a pity you must leave." He grimaced. "On a matter of national interest? You see, sir, the fact is that we haven't finished our *preparations* for her viewing. Ah ... perhaps early tomorrow?"

"No," I said.

Bile rose in my throat but couldn't kill the blood taste. I kept my stare fastened on him, polite, but edging toward anger. He began to crack under the pressure. Remfrey was one of those middle-aged men who can burst into a sweat and be completely drenched in a matter of seconds. He drew a handkerchief from his suit pocket and mopped his brow.

Strange to discover the loss welling inside me, and to realize I was no longer play-acting—the reality of my bond to Susan took over until I was telling the funeral director what I truly felt. "It's important for me not to let her go just yet. I have to see her face again and say a few last words to her. It's something she ..." I nearly said *wants*, "would have wanted me to do. It's something I must do."

He met my gaze. "Yes," he assented quietly. "I can see that, Mr. Prescott. Please wait here."

I didn't. I followed him along another hallway that zagged like lightning towards the back of the house. I could understand why the Vanderbilts had sold the place. The windows were too high—the top of the walls were lit with sunlight, but the rest of the rooms were left in darkness, with the shadows of trees stalking across the rafters. The gray was pervasive in a house now claimed by the dead. With a startled glance over his shoulder, Archibald Remfrey realized I walked in step behind him. We moved into another foyer, and he opened an unmarked door that led into the mortuary.

Remfrey spoke before I could see who he was talking to. "Mr. Standon, I have a ... ah, a somewhat unusual and *delicate* request to make that I sincerely hope you won't find ... uhm ... *too* unbecoming."

Standon rose like a reanimated cadaver, holding a hair brush. Bred on horror films, he was everything I stereotypically believed a mortician should be: tall, extremely gaunt, and pale. The one thing I didn't expect was the tenderness in his eyes, as if dealing with the dead only heightened his appreciation for life.

The center of my chest went numb when I realized he was "working" on Susan.

They'd laid her out on a metal table, hair perfectly done, a make-up kit open by her head. To her left was a tray filled with sharp instruments covered with fluid. I didn't want to look too long, for fear I'd steal one.

Two other bodies were on different enamel-topped tables, where large sinks and basins sat off to the sides. Being here, I felt as ghoulish as the other Follows, and immediately wanted to get away.

Remfrey introduced me and explained my supposed situation. Standon took it in stride with a shy smile, nodding in understanding. Discretion spurred Remfrey back to the door, but Standon remained at his station, silent, respectfully looking away from Susan's body, though a moment ago he'd been brushing her hair.

A sheet was drawn up over her breasts but fell in an unnatural pattern across her torso, where they'd had to reinforce her shattered rib cage for cosmetic purposes. I saw the thick, puckered scars weaving about her upper body and neck, and our rages twisted together, tightening once again, the infection of my back burning.

I tried to tell myself that whatever waited on the table, it wasn't Susan. I wanted Lowell Hartford to be right, that this could only be *the body*. Hopefully, she'd been released to a place where there was no need to fear the humiliation of being unable to heal.

I tried to force myself to believe it, but couldn't.

It was *Susan*.

In all her beauty and weakness and pain. I wanted at her again. My hand came up and moved to touch her, and I had to make a fist to keep from drawing the sheet aside to let me see the full extent of her scars.

Remfrey gave me one last awkward glance from the door and said, "I'll leave you for a few minutes, sir." He turned and gently closed the doors.

Comfortable with the situation, Standon still held the hair brush, running his finger back and forth along the bristles. He regarded me, started to say something, but thought better of it. His skin was the same pallor as Susan's, though the half applied make-up on her face added an eerie quality to her features. It took a few seconds to understand what was nagging me.

Standon had accented Susan's cheek bones with the rouge, and she looked very much like Jordan did when Jordan was trying not to look like Susan.

I held my fists at my sides. There should have been more. There should've been candlelight dinners and slow dancing on the veranda, breakfast in bed and lazy afternoons of love play—the romance you take for granted, putting it off, thinking, *someday, someday,* subduing the loneliness, running to your father's grave. Should've been, my God, what wasted words: weekends at Martha's Vineyard; rowboating in Belmont Park; winter nights devoted to cheddar popcorn and low-budget horror videos; and summer-carnival stuffed animals won for her by the brawn of her humble writer's arms, sending a sledge down against a clapper and clanging the bell. It should've been easy.

My heart thudded. The cold sweats chilled me the way the boulders at Montauk had on the night I'd met her; but my back burned. I watched her fall.

'Bye.

"You're not really her fiancé, are you?" Standon said.

"No."

It didn't faze him. The mortician grinned with serio-comic embarrassment, as if he hadn't meant to catch me in a lie. "You don't have the right look about you. There's no love there—not that everyone gets all emotional, of course." He shook his head. "But in you, it's something else."

"Bitterness, maybe."

"I don't believe so. I've been around enough misanthropes to know when I've met one." He smiled without showing teeth, the tight lines of his face deepening. "But I can understand, I surely can. She was a lovely girl, and beauty still comes through. It's my job to try to keep it there for awhile longer so anyone who cares can remember her like that, to the very end."

"It's a pleasant thought."

"Ain't it, though? You've got to keep a few nice precepts on hand at all times when you do what I do for a living." He took a breath, said, "Mind telling me what you are doing here?"

I needed to know. I turned to him. "I want to know about the scars. What can you tell me?"

On a nonverbal level, Standon already told me he was curious enough to accept me on my terms. He gestured abstractly. "They said she committed suicide."

"Yes."

He glanced across the room at the other bodies—an elderly man and woman—and his eyes flickered with effort as he put it together, thinking how some could struggle until they withered, and some could not.

"I had an Aunt Ellen who killed herself. She was younger than this girl. Story goes she was jilted at the altar after she'd already slept with the man. Fifty years ago that was considered the blackest shame." Words trailed off as he continued fingering the brush. "She left a long letter I never did read, but the skeleton rattling in my family closet says she was pregnant. In the middle of the Bible Belt that sin weighs heavily."

"Are you saying Susan was pregnant?" I asked.

"No, I was just relating a tale." Standon put the brush down and pointed to the scar weaving down her neck. His hushed voice was loud in the room. "Self-inflicted."

I nodded.

The thought had been perched at the back of my mind, but to hear him say it diffused the headache. "Are you positive?"

"Yes. I won't bore you with a discourse on the angle of knife-point entry and other jargon, but it's apparent if you know what you're looking at. I do. The ME must have spotted it, too." He massaged the bridge of his nose and said, "She was a sick girl, all right."

Except you don't get that kind of sick all on your own. I was through here and Standon knew it because he stepped aside and left the room to allow me a few seconds alone with Susan. She had the claws in too deep, and I wondered if I could have loved her if only we weren't coerced by circumstances into being sly and dangerous with one another. I thought I could have lived with waking up beside that face on my pillow every morning, listening to her telling llama jokes. What would have happened if, crying on the beach that night, she had confessed to me the things in her life that were worse than my mother's waffles? I coughed; I decided that no matter what odd looks Archibald Remfrey gave me, I'd return tomorrow for the funeral services. I had to see who was going to be there. I coughed again and reached out to pull the sheet over her face, or perhaps down so I could see her again, to know her the way I hadn't gotten to know her even in bed, but I was unable to do it. I couldn't mess up the hair Standon had been so lovingly brushing.

My throat was raw. I coughed again to clear it, and realized something was wrong. I spun and scanned the room: black-cotton smoke rolled under the door. I ran and carefully put my hand to the knob—it was hot. Christ. I unknotted my tie and wrapped it around my hand and tried the knob. The door was locked.

"Standon!" I shouted. "Remfrey!" I put my weight against it, slamming my shoulder into the mahogany. There was the crackling of fire directly outside, and farther down the corridor I heard choking, shouts and cries. Yellow flames licked out from the keyhole and around the borders of the door, hungrily reaching for me.

I wheeled and rushed the window, lifted a chair and threw it as hard as I could; the glass shattered, but the chair bounced back at me. There were iron bars on the outside of the window. Who the hell would want to break into a mortuary? I got to the sink and put my head under the faucet, took off my jacket, soaked it, and put it back on again. The old man and woman stared up at me with cotton-packed eyesockets.

The fire skimmed in under the door, igniting chemicals that had spilled onto the floor over the years. It came after my feet, alive, intelligent, and burning, like her. I hopped up onto the metal table with Susan. Tears dripped down my face as gusts of smoke came swirling inside. The consumption of the room was amazingly fast. There was a loud *crack* and part of the nearest wall buckled, plaster raining. I was getting high from lack of oxygen, and knew if I didn't do something fast they were going to have a closed casket for all of us.

I jumped off the table and tried to move it as the flames licked my legs; there were casters on the table that had never been used, but as I shoved hard against it, the table on which

Susan lay began to slowly roll. I aimed it at the door and pushed harder, swabbed by tongues of flame, squinting to see through the smoke, picking up speed. The sheet around her slipped off and was lost in the fire. I screamed from the heat, and at the last second, as her hair ignited, I dove and the table crashed through the door. Susan's body flopped sideways into the fire as gigantic gusts of flame poured into the room. It died down in the rush, and I covered my face and ran out.

I'd failed her again, and again she had died.

But, she saved me.

Standon lay crumpled in a circle of fire at the end of the hallway, arms splayed across the ring of flames; his hands were charred black, but I thought he might still be alive. I reached down and gripped him under the waist, lifted and flung him over my shoulder.

The fire itself was worse in the mortuary than in the funeral parlor, but the smoke remained the deadliest factor, billowing and mushrooming beautifully, insanely. I thought of the old lady's cigarette. I knew if I tripped and fell I'd lose what little breath I had left, take in a gulp of that polluted air and we'd all be dead. *Uh uh, c'mon.* I ran blindly, aiming for where I hoped the front door would be.

Windows exploded. I bounced into ceramic urns and statues of matronly angels. My pants cuffs and jacket were in flames, and the pain slapped as hard as my father, but there was no time to think about anything but movement. I ducked my head and bolted, doing my best to keep a tight hold on Standon. My lungs were ready to give.

Then something hard smashed into my face and I floundered backwards, the mortician out of my hands. I felt the cool wash of water spraying over me, putting out the flames that had caught my hair and clothes. Suddenly, I flopped down the slate steps on my back, with a jet stream of a high-powered hose going over my head. Hands gripped me under the shoulders as I began to pass out.

Faces leered at me in the blanketing smoke.

One of them was my father's.

Another was D.B.'s.

The one frowning, shaking his head at me, was Lieutenant Smithfield's.

7

Fiery faces gave way to hellish visions of Susan's flaming body riding atop me, digging nails into flesh, streaking me with a set of scars matching her own, insane eyes blazing.

Susan and I were on fire together, choking on one another as flames engulfed our bed. She giggled in a soothing, almost loving manner, urging me to hurt her. I did, once again, and always would so long as she asked. I wasn't sure how I managed it so effectively. We laughed as though lust and sorrow were the only lots we could afford to draw, the most human condition. Her face froze, with the sad smile, and melted into that of a nurse changing the dressings on my hands.

I groaned, and the nurse stared down impassively when she noticed I was awake.

"It's nice to have you back with us," she said, without a hint of sincerity. Some people don't like their jobs. "You're quite a lucky man. Just lie there and relax. You've had a nasty jolt." She handed me a glass of water and told me not to drink too quickly. I couldn't help it. She checked a bandage around my head; when her fingers probed the back of my neck I grunted, blinded with white pain.

"Jolt?" I echoed. My eyelids weighed a half ton each and gray spots had settled over my vision. I tried to blink the fog away but it wouldn't leave. "How long have I been out?"

"Twenty hours. Don't worry, the doctor will be in to explain everything to you." The nurse held up a clipboard and asked, "Do you feel nauseous?"

I wasn't about to shake my head. "No."

"Double vision?"

"You're a little blurry," I said.

"That's to be expected."

"Okay."

"You've got a mild concussion from where the fire hoses knocked you back against a slate step. Are you experiencing any acrid scents?"

"No. But I can't feel my fingers all that well."

"There's an anesthetic salve on them," she told me. "You have first degree burns on your hands and the backs of your legs. You're going to be fine, but right now you should try to get more sleep."

"I think you're right," I said, already fading, Susan tumbling into the flames and following me.

***

When I next awoke, Lieutenant Daniel Smithfield hovered over me, hands dug deeply in the pockets of his overcoat, butt of his gun visible in the jacket holster. The cold sweats hit, I had to piss, and my hands and legs throbbed painfully.

My mind raced with the amount of trouble I must be in. Smithfield would have checked up on me by now; he'd know about the Follows name. He'd know I'd lied to Remfrey and bullied my way in to view Susan's body. Since I was already under suspicion in her death, he'd be even more certain I was involved. Standon the mortician had been burned badly by the time they'd gotten him out of the fire; if he, or anyone else were hurt or dead, I'd be the prime suspect there, too. The suicide of a nineteen-year-old girl, which had never been tidy, would be even less so. I could imagine what he was thinking.

I didn't say anything.

Smithfield kept up his glare for another few seconds before allowing his gaze to wander over my bandages. He sat in the visitor's chair, hands still in his pockets, and leaned back against the radiator as hot water clanked through the pipes.

He began with a prelude. "At first I thought, okay, this guy is snorting a little coke with her, and they screw around for a while and things get out of hand, and he's got cum stains on his pants and she gets depressed and jumps because she's got too much money and she's bored. There's a higher suicide rate in the Hamptons than there is in a suburban ghetto like Wyndanch. It's a statistic I'll never understand, but it's one I've learned to deal with. So it's no great surprise when Lowell Hartford's daughter, who's got a juvie rap sheet that follows the usual pattern, winds up taking a swan dive out of her millionaire daddy's highest window. It's not even Christmas yet, and that's when the reports really start coming in, but October can be one of the ugliest months, too." He loosened the knot of his tie and undid the top button of his collar. His finger shot out to point at me. "Now you, you are a wiseass with a big mouth, and except for one drunk witness who needs a little therapy himself, I can't connect you to it. I have to ask the questions, so I ask them."

The radiator shut off at the exact moment Smithfield stopped speaking. The room was silent, footsteps filling the hall. I wanted to ask if I was under arrest, but restrained myself until he finished what he had to say. "It was my personal responsibility to inform Lowell Hartford that his youngest daughter is dead, by her own hand, and then my job is done and I get to go home and look at my five-year-old son sleep and worry about all the shit my wife doesn't like to hear me talk about, anymore. But before the paper work is even off my desk, I get a call from Hartford, and he tells me that the wiseass with the big mouth and cum stains has been nosing around his family, and it's not more than a couple of hours later before the fire department is rolling on a little barbecue over at White's Funeral Parlor."

"How is Standon?"

"Shut up until I'm finished." He waited a three count. "Dead. He was dead when you picked him up. But it wasn't the smoke that got to him, though that's what the paramedics thought when they finally gave up the CPR. He'd been struck across the top of his spine. Died of a broken neck. That mean anything to you?"

I finally realized the full scope of the darkness in Susan's life. The spectres were not only taking shape, they were already solid and on the move. They were killing. From out of her past, or out of mine. Harrison had told me I should treat the mystery like murder. Now I knew, in some fashion, that I was responsible for a man's death. Whoever set the fire had been trying to stop me, and Standon was murdered in my place.

I said, "I didn't do it."

Smithfield had no expression. "Tell me what you have to do with this. All of it."

I poured myself a glass of water. The anesthetic was wearing off and my hands were wracked with pain. The aches in my back, legs, and shoulders reminded me I had carried a dead man away from cremation, and that the Hartfords would never be able to view Susan one last time. Maybe she would have wanted it that way.

I told Smithfield everything from my night with Zenith Brite to the moment I hit the slate steps. I didn't abridge the story any, but it only took fifteen minutes to tell it all. He didn't care about reasons. Neither did I. I gave the facts, one after the other, the times, places, movements. My voice was the sound of a kettle drum, hollow and emotionless; it was my father's voice.

At the tail end of the tale the pretty but grumpy nurse came in, checked my pulse, felt the bumps on my head, and left a tray of food, promising that the doctor would be coming by in a few minutes.

"Everything you say matches up with what the Fire Marshal discovered," Smithfield told me. He said it as if he were certain I had conjured a cover story to fit the physical evidence.

I wondered when he would mention the dead children.

"No witnesses to anything?" I asked.

"Just the statements I've taken from Remfrey and the widow Torrasino. They didn't see anyone but you."

Of course not. The fire was rushing everywhere, the heat following me. "So what happens now?" I asked.

I believed he would arrest me; it made sense. When I was writing my first Jacob Browning novel, I'd quizzed Jack at length about police procedure, asking him what the police would do in any number of circumstances. He told me "Cops arrest everybody. It's not our job to decide whether someone is guilty. We drag them into court and it's up to the judge, prosecutor, and the defending lawyer to decide who stays and who goes." I doubted if Francis Meachum would represent and defend me to the fullest of his capabilities.

Smithfield stood to hover over me again. "I've done some checking on you, Follows," he said. "Let's say that I believe you, for the moment. I know about your brother the child killer, and about your father's trial. I hope that shit don't really run in the family, because if it does I'll take you out like a dog. You've been chasing shadows and stepping on toes all over the Island."

"And you're going to sit back and watch what happens."

He nodded, re-buttoned his collar, and straightened his tie. "Remember what I said."

I would.

***

After I hobbled back from the the lavatory, ready to eat, the doctor came in and examined me; he was small, stooped, and wore black horn-rimmed glasses, and I kept waiting for him to break into Groucho's funny walk. Unlike the nurse, his smile never left his face.

I bit through my lip when he unwrapped the bandages to take a closer look at the burns. Stomach muscles contracting, shriek in the middle of my throat, I couldn't fully comprehend what kind of self-hatred had forced Susan into willingly undergoing such agony. I thought she'd gone for the quick kill, jumping out the window, getting it all over in one instant—that I could understand. But God, how I'd been wrong. She'd been dying slowly before that, just a piece of flesh at a time, a cut, a slice, a slash.

The grumpy nurse looked even less friendly than before. She handed the doctor wet sponges, which he used to swab down the raw wounds and blisters.

"Good, there's no infection," he said. "But your back, that's another story. I had to lance and clean out some nasty lacerations. You should have gone to a doctor days ago." He gave me a reprimanding sneer, knowing what had caused the scratches. "I don't think there's any danger from such a mild concussion. If you notice any strange scents or sounds or anything affecting your vision, I want you to buzz for the nurse immediately."

"I want to get out of here as soon as possible."

He took his glasses off and chewed on one plastic arm. "I'd like to keep you under observation for at least a couple more days."

"No, I want to leave in the morning."

The burns hurt badly at the moment, and a headache snuck out from the brush and came on strong, pounding heavier by the minute. It was a good idea to stay the night. "Who did you notify?"

"We got hold of your friend ... uhm ... Harry? Others have been by several times over the past two days, but the police lieutenant refused to allow anyone in until he talked with you first. As a matter of fact, I believe there's someone waiting now. Visiting hours are over, but we'll make an exception under these circumstances."

He shambled out, the grumpy nurse following. Jack and Carrie entered a minute later, arguing. I hoped she hadn't confessed the truth to him. They were holding hands, a sure sign they'd had a blow-out and were in the process of making up, or pretending to make up; Carrie was much better at covering her feelings than Jack.

Surprisingly, he wore his police uniform. I'd only seen him in it three or four times in the five years he'd been on the force. He must have either just gotten off his shift and come straight to the hospital from Brooklyn, or he was on for night duty. His six one, two-twenty frame took up the entire doorway so that Carrie had to slip in behind him in order to remain holding hands. They managed it.

Carrie glowed with concern and curiosity, making eye contact that bemoaned affairs. She was dying to ask a million questions, but I could see Jack had already told her not to grill me at the moment.

"How ya doing, buddy?" he asked.

"Hanging in," I said. The tray of hospital food was the most unappetizing substance I'd ever seen in my life—like a TV dinner that hadn't been thawed out correctly—but I couldn't care less. I didn't bother to identify any of it before I ate.

"Hanging in," Carrie repeated. "For an author you aren't much for detail."

"I'm alive and I itch and I'm constipated."

"Better," she said. "But none of it seems to have affected your appetite much."

"After being weaned on my mother's waffles everything else tastes good by comparison."

Jack laughed. "I'll keep that in mind the next time you drop by for dinner and you bitch because I like my veal cutlets well done. And when there's no beer in the fridge."

"Beer is another matter completely."

The grin dropped, inch by inch like a weight too heavy too hold up. His mouth thinned as he took a serious tone, eyes brimming with anger and fear. "Are you sure you're really okay, buddy?"

Carrie breathed, "Jesus, those bandages ..."

"It looks worse than it is," I said, hating to sound cliché, caught with a mouthful of orange-tasting brown stuff.

Jack made one of her "hmph" sounds, and I couldn't remember which of them had taught it to the other. Two fat tears slid down her cheeks, and she bent and gave me a kiss on the forehead, then turned to leave the room.

"Don't tell Linda, Carrie."

Being haunted by one ghost was enough.

"I already did," she said, "but I don't think she's going to come. Not that you'd care." She sobbed harder, covered her nose, and fled.

"You want to bring me up to speed?" Jack asked.

Speed was something I hoped to avoid until I found the right direction to move. "What has Harrison told you?"

"The basic gist, but as Carrie mentioned, you authors aren't much for giving details. I know about the party you went to, and the girl you were talking about. I'm sorry."

It hit me all wrong that someone should be sorry—apologizing to me—for Susan's death. "How long have you been here?"

"Stopped in twice yesterday and once this morning. I've got the night shift again so I've got to cut out in a few minutes, but I wanted to try again. This time we got the evil eye from that lieutenant."

"See anybody waiting around you didn't know?"

"A tall blond with dimples that outshine Shirley Temple. She arrived the minute Carrie and I walked in here."

Jordan. "No one else?"

"No, why?"

"Did anyone feed my dogs?"

"Carrie did. She got the manager to open up your flat." He frowned. "This isn't exactly what I'd call bringing me up to speed."

I could tell he was wondering just how bad my concussion

had been. Talking about a killer would impress him, I thought, the way talking about book contracts would impress Harrison: it was a part of the life's work. Jack had hardened in his years on the force, but he'd also weakened, like me, changed to a point where the two of us could not relate on certain subjects. There were things he would mention in passing but never actually tell me; I did the same. I wanted him in my corner when I went back to shake the Hartford tree, but I understood he could do little to protect me from Smithfield, or anybody else.

"Sorry, Jack," I said, though I wasn't, not about being unable to bring him up to speed; I wasn't sure I was sorry about sleeping with Carrie, either. He'd had his share of ladies on the side, and spoke of them as conquests, wearing them like medals. I couldn't talk to him about this.

Jack stared intently at me, the frown gone, replaced by something else resembling shame. Before I could say anything more Jordan walked into the room. I swung my head around to look at her and a sudden lightning bolt flared behind my eyes. I smiled wanly at her, and Jack was kind enough to make his farewell quickly.

"We'll talk more later," he said. "Tomorrow morning."

"I'll be checking out."

"I'll catch up with you at your place, then."

"Okay," I said. He moved to leave, and yet, because there was something happening around us we couldn't completely grasp, I was compelled to throw his own words back at him. "You two have a nice thing going," I said. "She's a special lady." For some reason, it was the wrong thing to say.

He stepped by Jordan without a sidewards glance.

She smiled at me and said, "I don't suppose 'Hey good lookin', what's cookin'? would go over big right now, huh?"

She had her sister's sense of puns. "A lot better than one would think."

Jordan Hartford wore white jeans and a gray, heavy wool sweater which still managed to show off each of her athletic contours. Rather than California wild, she looked as if she should be queen of the winter carnival, soft and ephemeral. The breeze beat at the windows, and she started at the sound of the rattling glass. I'd never look at a window in the same way, either.

I'd eaten too quickly and the food wasn't settling right, and the pain was making me sweat; I shifted in the bed, unable to find a comfortable position. I couldn't tell what was going on behind the dimpled, bright smile. My usually competent intuition was failing me more and more, the headache hammering away until it was difficult to see straight. Unreadable currents swirled.

Jordan had switched off again; the scared little girl she'd been with her father was completely gone. Now she was cool and in control. "I like your haircut," she said. A quick peek in the lavatory mirror showed that half an inch had been singed from my head. "It's a little uneven in spots, but my friend Maurice could fix that for you. He's a wonderful stylist and can do magic with short hair."

"You'll have to give me his number," I said.

She went to give my curls a tousle but the bandage stopped her. "I want to thank you for helping me with my father. You were brave to stand up to him the way you did, and I think he respects you for it."

I doubted that. "I don't much respect a man who strikes his own daughter."

"It was barely a love tap, and he was terribly sorry. Strange, but that made me feel good. I was almost glad when he hit me, you know? It was like I had something physical over him, not merely ... uhn ... *rampant* fear. Does that sound odd?" She made a pouty face. "It sounds weird to me."

"No." I thought of Susan drawing a knife across her own body, the edge of the blade cutting deeper and deeper as she dug it in, doing to herself what D.B. did to others. *Dig me.* What could sound odd anymore?

"What were you doing at the funeral home, Nathaniel? You asked me about scars, but so far as I know, she didn't have any, so why? What were you talking about? What happened to my sister?"

My skin was suddenly slick and clammy. "I think you should get out of town for a while, Jordan."

"What?"

"Stay away from Sutter and the Fat Ernies and anyone else who was at Susan's party. Your father told the truth. They're not your friends." The back of my legs stung like mad, and I had to shift onto my left side, my back hot but no longer itching; I was starting to wrack. "At least one of them isn't."

Jordan opened her purse and wiped my face with a wad of tissues. "Oh god, Nathaniel, you've become so pale in the last minute. I'm going to call a doctor."

"I just need some rest."

But she called for the doctor anyway, and the grumpy nurse checked my pulse and my pupils and brought me a couple of pain relievers. She told Jordan she had to leave and stood there with her arms crossed until Jordan said good-bye.

"I'll stop back in tomorrow."

"No. Call me when you're someplace safe." She was pale too, I noticed, and then her face shimmered like snow falling through the empty, ice-covered branches of trees. "Be careful," I said, and passed out again.

***

Harrison arrived at ten in the morning with a loose-fitting sweat suit for me; I wasn't going to be able to wear a pair of jeans over the bandages around my legs. As it was I could barely walk, and every time I took a step I felt the blisters pulling tautly, threatening to rip open my calves and thighs. I signed the proper forms and—because of hospital policy—had to be brought out the front door in a wheelchair, which hurt like hell. The grumpy nurse grinned like crazy when she was rid of me. Maybe she enjoyed her job after all.

Harrison had picked up my car from White's Funeral Home and brought it back to my flat. I couldn't keep up with him as we crossed the parking lot to his Honda CRX. He stopped, unsure of whether he should assist me. "It'll be a while before I'm up for one of our runs."

"You wanted to stir things up."

He opened the passenger door for me. I scuttled in. CRX's are small two-seaters, but there was plenty of leg room, which I was grateful for. I tried to put on the seat belt, but couldn't work my hands deftly enough to snap it around me. He reached over and made sure it locked.

"So?" he said.

Before I realized I'd begun to say anything I was already talking, I didn't know what drove me to explain this side of things to him. I had no control over myself. Seething, I wanted whoever had pushed Susan into mutilating herself. I wanted the firebug who had destroyed her body and murdered Standon. There was no way to contain the rage. It ripped over me, happy to be home again. Drivers in traffic stared at me in wide-eyed amazement. My skull was flaring red now, not white, the frustration building like a tidal wave in the car. I almost talked about my brother.

Harrison handled it like a pro, something you could always count on. He drove impassively, relaxed but vigilant. I sat catching my breath, bandaged hands out before me like a monkey without a cup.

"You're okay now," he said. It wasn't a question.

"Yes," I said, uncertain.

He wasn't going to talk about my purgative tantrum; he'd wait until some night a long time from now, go over it with the fine-toothed comb of human scrutiny, and then write about it in his Poe book. He knew better than to dwell, and sought to affirm. "Seems like you pissed somebody off."

I nodded. "Didn't expect him to come at me the way he did. Or so soon."

"Narrows down your choices though. Richie Sutter is probably your man."

"I don't think so. He wouldn't do it like this. Too risky, too blatant. Sutter might not be a genius, but subtlety is his specialty. You can feel how hard he works at being invisible. I have nothing on him and he knows it; I didn't even manage to rile him. He had no reason to take such a chance."

He thought about it as we pulled up to my apartment complex. "So who else is there?"

"Anyone at the party. Somebody's either been tailing me from the start or else was watching the Hartford home and decided to follow me after I left the other afternoon."

"Her father, possibly."

"Yes," I said. "Possibly."

"Or some kind of a real whack job. Maybe he was planning on setting the fire the whole time and you just stumbled into it, and he figured to take you out for the hell of it, or didn't care. Maybe he just wanted to scar her more."

He pulled up in front of my flat. I got out of his car into the chill October air. Elms would be banging against my windows like the children wanting to be let in. You could smell Halloween approaching.

The season of masks.

And tricks.

***

The dogs went wild when they saw me; it took everything I had not to fall over as they leaped. Being a full grown husky, Achilles was large enough so his paws landed on the center of my chest when he jumped, but Ulysses was still a pup and kept circling my legs with excited wiggles. I was scared he'd brush me the wrong way. After a minute I let them out back. My answering machine had four hang-ups, a computerized voice telling me I'd won a free vacation, and Carrie. I replayed her message twice, but each time she said the same thing, her voice soft from strain. "*I know Jack is sleeping with somebody else. That's why I was willing to let you get at me, besides it being so good.*"

A half hour later there was a knock on the door.

I opened it and recognized him immediately: the guy named John who hadn't shaken my hand at the party, and who'd later wandered off to Susan's bedroom when I told him to call for an ambulance.

There were dark bags under his eyes. His greasy hair was uncombed and knotted. Where he had been thin and wiry before, he now seemed starved, hastily shaved cheeks sunken in, dappled with stubble.

He said, "I read about what happened to you in the papers. About the fire and Susan." He gagged on her name and nothing else came out for a few seconds. His mouth worked soundlessly.

"What is it?"

"You need my help and I need yours."

He wavered as though something had finally caught up with him and he didn't have the strength to defend himself any longer. He'd show me the face of the beast I was hunting.

8

I didn't like the fact he'd found me at my place less than an hour after I'd checked out of the hospital. I wasn't in much shape for a fight, but I could smash the mirror on the wall if forced to. I stood close enough to pull shards.

Thinking about what he'd said, searching for any sign connecting him to the fire, all I needed was a glimmer of venom, some self-satisfied curl of his lip or hidden laugh in his squint.

Nothing.

Wind chipped the lawn, smoothing grass like a hand pressing down. Neighborhood kids rollerbladed up the sidewalk, carrying home paper sacks from Leggino's Deli around the block. John didn't turn as they skated behind him, laughing loudly. Leaves kicked at his ankles. He had the same emotionless expression as the night he'd walked off towards Susan's bedroom after Jordan had passed out in my arms. Beneath the thick lenses, his eyes were faraway and cold as shale.

"I loved her," he said.

"Who are you?"

"My name is John Brackman. I was Susan's ... friend." He spoke hesitantly, unsure of his footing. "I like to think I was her boyfriend, but it's not true, not really. Not at the end, anyway. Whatever. We were very close for a time. During the spring."

Detachment had already come and gone for him; the same as anyone who's held on to a struggling lover out of fright, fearing loneliness, only to eventually sputter, drown, and then, perhaps, bob again. It doesn't always happen. Brackman was learning to live with loss, disgusted by his own weakness and needs, filling the void with too much of something that would never completely fit. Not with hatred or lust, the way most of us found our fulfillment. He took on the role of tragic figure.

A faint swirl of pathos lurked among his frozen eyes. "May I come in, Mr. Follows?"

"Yes."

He stepped past me, and I shut the door. He couldn't decide whether to sit on the couch or in a recliner across the living room. After a half minute of hesitation he chose the couch, and I drew up my desk chair beside him. He wasn't one for action, but activity was his reason for entering. A horror movie scenario seemed to be playing out: vampires must be invited inside.

"Why did you come here?" I asked.

"I told you. I need your help."

"You also said I needed yours. What did you mean by that?"

One word followed another like the faltering footsteps of a dying man. Everything about him was lethargic. Even the pop of the pulse in his neck appeared to be too slow. "Susan and I met at the Community Cinema Complex back in February. Ever been there?" He wasn't asking. "They were running a Bergman retrospective: *The Seventh Seal* and *Fanny and*

Alexander. I was late getting there and the theater was packed. Mostly with older couples who don't need thirty million dollars of special effects to appreciate a film. It's a tiny auditorium and doesn't sit many, not like the Multiplexes. The lights were dimming by the time I found my seat." He rubbed his chin, slowly, growing slower. "You know how when you're in an elevator no one looks at anyone else? The same's true in movies. It was forty-five minutes into *The Seventh Seal* before I realized how beautiful the girl was I'd sat beside."

Romance can infiltrate the substance of speech even when the speaker has no intention of allowing it to surface; nothing changed in the flat tone of his voice, but I sensed the poetry Brackman wanted to bring forward.

He went on to mention the first words he and Susan Hartford had exchanged: they were memorable only to him, the way llama jokes would only be funny to me. An ambiguous jealousy flashed through my nerves when he told of the kissing and making angels in the snow, bouquets of flowers and Shoebox Greetings cards. I felt strangely vindicated when he admitted they'd never slept together.

There are mythmakers and mythtakers. Brackman was a taker; he took Susan's memory and bought himself a goddess. He spoke with all the loose lust and love he'd made do without until she'd given him the hope of something more. Whether it was real or not didn't matter—it was hope, even now. I could see just how high on a pedestal he'd already placed her. I had no doubt that, in death, she'd ascended farther.

He told me of her beauty as if I'd never laid eyes on her, chattering on about her wit, kindness, and gentleness. The pulse in his throat beat a bit faster; I could see his heart. He talked about, and to, her spirit. He actually used the word "indominatable." My grandmother would have called it gumption; Francis Meachum would have said Susan was just being selfish and willful, but he would have meant something else that I still had to find out about.

Brackman commended the unbreakable spirit he didn't recognize when it came raining down from the window and shattered on the patio like a glass swan. I listened as he mentioned museums and arboretums, Lincoln Center and Circle in the Square. It brought a new light to Susan Hartford, but not a new reality. She searched for a reason to live while dancing steadily towards the edge.

Towards me.

What he said explained the odd mixture of gatherers at her party. Originally I'd believed them all to be acquaintances of Jordan. Lowell Hartford had made the same assumption and mistake. Instead, the divided lifestyles were the ends of Susan's spectrum folded in upon itself. What drugs and juvenile abandon did not yield, neither did art, classical music, intimate conversations, or sex.

Brackman rambled for half an hour; I didn't interrupt to ask questions or make comments. After the first fifteen minutes he more or less became oblivious to my presence, lost in his own private myth, some of which I shared. For him, Susan was the embodiment of unrequited love, a martyr to whom he could safely give his adoration. He finished the good fight, paying his price for every what-might-have-been and never-was. He slumbered in a satisfying dream.

All writers go through first drafts, every artist begins with a sketch. I realized he was simply the original mold for myself, an earlier model Susan had discarded.

Their relationship lasted only a few months. Brackman

said he didn't know why it ended, but a twinge of memory
blew his eyes wide and made his nostrils flare. It was clear he
still could not fully believe it was over. Although he tried
several more times to meet with Susan, she resisted his attempts. He ran into her twice at The Bridge during the summer, while she was with her sister and other men; she remained warm and friendly, and seemed genuinely glad to see
him, but had shown no desire to pick up where they'd left
off. He hadn't spoken with her for ten weeks when she invited
him to her party, gathering the flock.

After he'd finished his reminiscing, Brackman sat flushed
and empty, staring dizzily at the walls of my apartment. I
couldn't see him living much longer without professional help.
Suicide had captured his sense of loyalty, and I could see him
leaping to his own death not long from now, an errant knight
chasing his princess off the tower.

"Her father was screwing her," he said. "You must know
that."

He was deadpan. No vehemence surged in his voice, no
hurt. There wasn't even very much belief; I got the feeling he
was trying to convince himself that what he'd just told me
was true. The image stuck, though.

*"I would never hurt you," he, my father, said, taking me in his
hand, and hurting me.*

"What makes you think Hartford sexually abused her?" I
croaked. I cleared my throat. The picture came clear, but that
didn't make it truth. But, considering the conversation I'd
had with Harrison, a part of me understood exactly how much
sense it made—those sins possibly writhing beneath Lowell
Hartford's granite exterior, like my own father.

But another side could not conceive the idea. Regardless

of how good or evil a man he might actually be, I thought Hartford was too strong to ever give in to any perverse urges that would call for the use of a child, much less his own daughter. Susan had told me her parents were great people, and there had been no fear or anger. Yet Jordan was terrified of him.

Brackman stirred and raised his chin from his chest. He looked as if I were a teacher who'd asked a question he didn't know the answer to; it was the only animation he'd shown.

"What makes me think that? Because it makes sense, that's why. Because she lived with terror. Something festered inside her like a bullet gone septic. Whenever I asked her about it she'd put up a wall. She was good at putting up walls and compartmentalizing her life. She could put her feelings in boxes on a shelf and store them away. It must've taken half her life to learn to do that, making those walls so much a part of who she was. It has to have something to do with that bastard. He must have refused to let her to see me anymore." Brackman flew now, forgetting her as he spoke of her, remembering only selfishness and needing to stake the blame. "I wasn't good enough for his baby daughter. No middle class trash accountant would do for a son-in-law. He didn't want anyone else to have her because he wanted her for himself, the sick bastard. You know that."

Her walls may have been fortified, but his were already tumbling. I didn't like the way he said "You know that."

"What do you want from me, John?"

"I saw you at The Bridge the other night talking with Richie Sutter."

"Have you been following me?"

"No, but you're in the middle of everything. At the party with Susan and Jordan. And then sitting at Richie Sutter's

own private table, drinking with him and that singer. Why?"
He pointed at me and tapped the air with his finger, gaining
an odd momentum. "You were with Susan when she died. A
couple of days ago I picked up the paper only to see your
name splashed across the front page, with a photo of White's
Funeral Home burning down. They had a story about your
brother." He blanched, and swallowed hard, searching me as
if he could spot faulty genetics. I got him a beer and he drank
it in three pulls, dribbling on his shirt. He didn't know what
to make of me, but was asking for my help, anyway.

"I still don't know what you want."

He said, "I want to know what happened. I want to know
if Hartford paid you off—" His hand moved from where it
was resting on his knee, moving up to unbutton his coat. He
acted no faster than he talked. "To kill her and burn the body
so that no one else would be able to see what kind of a sadistic
maniac he is, how he scarred her."

A heat in his voice peaked on the word "sadistic" and
then faded under his breath. I'd been watching a man trying
to generate a fury he did not feel, priming himself on decep-
tions he was too intelligent to believe. His motives were suddenly apparent.

Susan had a good eye for men: Brackman and I were alike
in many ways, not the least of which being we were both
romantics in our vastly different, faulty fashions. My understanding of him crystallized in that second. I almost smiled
at the irony when I saw his fragment of the picture.

Leaping out of my chair, I was on him in an instant. The
clack of his teeth was explosive as I slammed my fist across
the hinge of his jaw. The burns shrieked. Brackman didn't
make a sound as he went sprawling across the arm of the

couch. His glasses flew off and clattered against my computer keypad. I set up to hit him again, but the fight was already out of him—it had never been there to begin with.

A thin track of blood dripped from the corner of his mouth. I turned him over, opened his coat, and patted his pockets down. "Where is it?"

"Uhn."

"Where is it?"

He touched his bleeding lip and dropped his fist across the folds of his coat. I smacked his hand away and yanked the coat open, reached in and pulled out a pint-sized .22 caliber pistol, my brother's second choice over his preferred blades.

Gaining control of myself was difficult, the cooing in my ear loud and wet. I backhanded him, emptied the gun, and threw it in his lap. "Idiot."

"Who are you?" he asked.

"I want to find out what happened to her as much as you do, Brackman. I wasn't hired by her father to kill her, and I'm not so sure Hartford abused her, though it's possible. If he did, I may kill him myself and I don't want you in the way. You were right, I do need your help. You're going to help me fill in more of the blanks."

"Who are you?" he asked again, face screwed. I found his glasses on my desk and gave them back. "Why were you with her?"

His questions annoyed me; he'd come here to play avenging angel, yet his own rationality refused to let him get away with it. I didn't especially feel like being civil anymore. "Listen, I was nearly barbequed a couple days ago. I'm in no mood for your shit. I was her friend, too." It was a lie, I supposed, but he would want to believe me. Rollerblading kids whizzed by the front window and the dogs barked happily in the yard. "You said you'd never been to bed with her, so how do you know about the scars?"

His face reddened. He sucked in his cheek and began chewing. He waited. I smacked him again, feeling the blisters ripping open beneath my bandages.

"Goddamn you, tell me."

No fear; there wasn't enough left inside of him to be afraid. He was nearly dead for her. He enjoyed his pain as much as she'd enjoyed hers. Brackman grinned inanely at me. "I took her to the Chateau la Mer. Even with reservations we had to wait at the bar for an hour before a table opened up. I was angry because I wanted it to be a special night." The momentum carried. "I wanted to make love to her. We were drinking steadily, more than usual. We were bored. By the time our entrees were served she was wasted. I was crocked, too, but not nearly as bad. We were laughing. When we left I had to drag her to the parking lot, and the valet attendants helped me get her into the car. We drove down to the Lindenhurst Marina to get some fresh air."

"And you raped her," I finished.

"*No*," he lied. We both had to lie about her.

"You took advantage of her while she was too out of it to resist."

"No, you pig, it wasn't like that. We slid the seat back and fell asleep holding each other and staring out at the bay. A couple hours later she shifted and woke me. I was still a little drunk and thought she wanted to make love. I wanted her so badly." Jealousy snared him. "You don't understand! She was awake and lying across my chest, looking out at the moon, and we started kissing and touching. It was dark. I couldn't see anything in the car, but after her blouse was off I ... felt ... she was layered with welts and scars." His breathing became a machine-gun staccato, and sweat pooled in the middle of his upper lip. "Christ, she was disfigured."

Clearly, part of what had driven him this far was guilt over his actions. Once again, I was stung to see just how similar the trails we'd walked with Susan were.

"Is that when your relationship ended?"

"No. Yes. I was ... revolted by what I saw. I couldn't help it, I couldn't. She knew the truth, and to this day I believe she was glad for it. Things had already begun to dissolve. I'd wanted her to give more, but she wouldn't consider any kind of a real commitment. I thought her father was putting pressure on her because I'm not on the Forbes top fifty. Sex became a big issue, a reason to argue." He got squirrely on the couch. "Who can stand that loneliness? Who's going out with a lady who won't ever let you sleep with her? I didn't know what it meant or why it was happening. She was doing a lot more coke by then." He couldn't continue with that chain of thought. He licked his blood. "Layers."

I said, "I know."

He glared at me, both of us jealous over a dead girl we never knew, but who understood us so intimately in our failures.

"Who did it?" he asked. You could see him twisting the thoughts, pulling and pushing them like a child playing with clay, sculpting them into a shape he could get his hands around. "Hartford?"

"You knew her better than me," I said. "Tell me what Susan's life was like when you first met her. Who was she with at the Bergman retrospective?"

Brackman's lips skinned back from his teeth. "Richie."

I could see Sutter and his entourage taking up three rows of the Community Cinema, his pearly animal smile going off like a flash in the darkness. "What do you know about him?"

That registered. Forehead furrowed as he slipped backwards to The Bridge and those nights he'd seen Susan out with other men, he grimaced as if trying to break his concentrated hate loose from Lowell Hartford so he could spread it onto Richie Sutter.

"If you want something, he has it."

"More than cocaine."

He chuckled dryly. "According to Susan, he has everything. All kinds of drugs, and he's probably into a whole lot of other shit as well. Maybe pimping or gambling or pornos. Susan never came right out and said it, but she implied as much. I honestly don't know."

"How close was she to him?"

"It was weird. We spent a lot of time in his club. There was always a good band playing, excellent food. For a while I thought she and Sutter were seeing each other, but later on I thought he and Jordan were lovers. They would sometimes make out during the night, and she left with him a few times. They weren't friends, but there was—" Brackman searched for the word, came up empty, "you know, something. Jordan was part of the circuit. Dependent on atmosphere. It was hard to tell the difference between flirting and anything more. Jordan hit on most of the guys, but that was her personality. Smiles and flashy, sexy dresses. She had a lot to prove. Dirty dancing and giggling at everything some guy said. She liked hanging around with the bouncers after the club closed."

Sutter and Jordan were other orbits. He was right, there was something. "Did you and Susan go there often?"

"In the beginning, in February. Then we sort of left most of that behind. She'd never been to the Museum of Modern Art before, so I took her there. She enjoyed plays and foreign movies. We went to dinner theaters and cafes. A few times we went with Sutter and Jordan." Brackman was tired of talking and getting vague in his answers, refining the past through a rose-colored filter.

A sacrifice can become envious even of that status.

"Stay away," I told him. "Don't let Susan suck you into the grave after her."

"I loved her."

"I believe you."

The pistol was still in his lap. He fumbled with it and then carefully placed the gun back in his pocket. I gave him the bullets and he put them in a different pocket. "What are you going to do, Follows?"

He stood up, drained and physically weak. I knew he wouldn't bounce back and find another girl. He didn't have the faith to strive forward. He didn't have enough rage to keep him in motion.

As he stepped outside, he turned and said, "*Who are you?*"

I shut the door.

9

I swallowed two painkillers and waited for them to take effect; it didn't happen quickly enough so I took another. After twenty minutes the tolling in my head and the aching of the burns began to fade.

The kids playing out front squealed and skated home as it began to drizzle. Ulysses yawped at the door, stuck his nose to the jamb and sniffed. Achilles hoped to give chase, and I let them in. Laughter perked their ears.

I fixed myself lunch and ate without tasting. The dogs sat staring intently at my plate, chins following the food to my mouth. Ulysses made tight figure eights under the table, and Achilles gave me a stolid, wolfish leer. I missed Homer, my blind bassette hound; I missed what he represented almost as much.

The rain pounded harder. Water throbbed beneath the panes. One of the kitchen windows was open about an inch, and the bottom of the curtains swayed and danced, swept by the breeze like a flirtatious lady's dress. Ulysses stood on his hind legs and pirouetted along with them, boxing the air with his front paws.

I uncapped a bottle of beer, knowing how foolish it was to drink after the painkillers. Pushing my luck had become another vice. I called Carrie; after the fourth ring her answering machine picked up. The batteries were running down, which added a thick and slurred timbre to her voice.

"It's me," I said. "I'll be home all day if you want to talk."

She wouldn't. I laid down and stared at the ceiling for five minutes, clutching for a handful of ties: the dead children, Homer, Susan. I was more attached to the dead than I was to the living. I took another painkiller and re-read the opening chapters of the novel I'd begun on the beach; Jacob Browning's actions were fake, hollow, and falsely macho. I couldn't distinguish what I was reading as something I had written myself. It would sell if I ever finished it.

I went through the piles of mail, hoping to re-establish the fact I had a life outside the events after Montauk. *Uh huh.* Common practices had vanished into background. Envelopes splayed across the bed. I left them there and went through the papers. I didn't want to read rejections.

The news had the details of White's Funeral Home correct, and I was surprised to see there was no particular slant taken. I had not been made out to be a criminal, a victim, or an alleged murderer posing as the fictitious Paul Prescott; if anything, I was cited as being a heroic good samaritan risking my life to save Standon. He was described as having died from injuries sustained in the fire. Questions put to Archibald Remfrey were answered succinctly and to the point, yet he didn't add much about me.

Either Lieutenant Smithfield wasn't releasing information to the press in the hopes of ferreting out the murderer, or else Lowell Hartford had collected a debt in order to keep the story low-key. Perhaps Hartford was through allowing his daughter's memory to make pulp news, and wanted to let her rest in peace, if she could. She couldn't, and if he knew her at all, he'd know that. Maybe he had, in fact, driven her out the third story window of his own home and hired someone to trail and kill me. Or maybe John Brackman had set the fire himself, stupid, twisted, heartbroken fool that he was.

The beer and pills caught up, settling over me like mosquito netting. I took another pill; I wondered if it would be enough to kill me. The urge to run returned. I fought the need to flee. The past pulled at my ankles like the hands of children, like the draw of the sea until I was left rolling and gasping in the surf. Nostalgia flared. I swallowed two more pills. I wanted to see Linda, hold her for a time, play with Randy and wrestle with them across the carpets the way we once had, Ninja Turtles and Power Rangers and Batman action figures ready to attack. "No, llama lips, no! Get away!" If I simply closed my eyes, I could be there again in my mind. *I would never hurt you.* The raindrops chattered, pleading for entrance as much as I wanted to find a way out. I took another pill and finished the beer.

***

Fog.

Grit.

Pulled from a deep blackness tinged with ocean blue, rising from the bottom of a wet pit in the backyard. I gagged and hacked deep in my chest. I was blind. My mother warned me this would happen.

No, it was dark. Thrashing from dreams I didn't remember, but could guess at, I'd wound up with my face buried under the sheets neatly wrapped around me like thread on a spool. I began to untangle myself when I realized it was the ringing of the phone that had awakened me.

I got free from the comforter and fumbled for the alarm clock before I reached for the phone: it was 6:10. I checked the windows to see if it was morning or evening.

Evening. In the living room, the answering machine had already picked up and I could hear a girl's quiet voice leaving a message. I lifted the receiver and interrupted.

"Nathaniel?" said Jordan. "Is that you?"

I cleared my throat. "Yes."

"You sound like hell. Did I wake you?"

"No."

"I'm sorry. I guess I should have waited before I rang, but I was worried. You looked so ill yesterday I didn't think they could possibly release you. You should have stayed until you'd recovered. Why did you leave so early? What are you trying to prove?"

"Where are you?" I said. "How are you?"

"Crazy." She giggled. "*Crazy*." She savored the word, tasting its flavor. Jordan found it did the job well. She laughed louder, that same high and winding titter that made my fillings ache. I thought she was about to go into another talking jag. "Yeah, yeah, I'd have to say that about covers it. I think I'm inching towards the other end of the pool. You never know when you ..." She put the skids on. The pause lengthened into a somber silence. "We have a lot to talk about," she whispered. "Don't we?"

This brew was boiling over. Susan seemed to be saying, *Take my sister since you couldn't have me.* Maybe I'd known that from the beginning. The picture was coming together like fragments of a mirror, or torn sections of a map; I didn't know what would turn up at **X**, what I'd see in the mirror. None of us did. I had the tail of an animal—one with several heads and hands, some already dead, some still living—and the harder I held on the deeper it bit. It was time to break the thing's back.

"Yes," I said. "We have to talk."

"Well, you were right," she said. "I have to get out of town for a while. My mother's in a valium daze all day long, every day. There's nothing I can do to help her. We don't talk; we don't leave the house. I'm not even sure she eats anymore. My father seals himself in his study and works twenty hours a day on the phone and sleeps in a hall chair. The doorbell rang incessantly until he clipped the wires. We're in our own fall-out shelter, hiding underground. We've got people stopping over all day long: reporters; my dad's business partners and clients; museum people; but nobody gets in. I don't know what the hell is happening anymore. I need time away from here, but ... Nathaniel, I don't want to be alone."

Who was being offered up?

"No," I told her.

"I haven't said anything yet."

"You don't have to."

"I think I do," she whispered. "Will you come stay with me for a few days in the city? Until I clear my head a little and start getting a handle?"

"No, I don't think that would be too good for either of us."

She snorted. "Why?"

Because, I thought, it's what your sister wanted.

I could hear her switching the receiver from ear to ear, her hair brushing over the mouthpiece with a soft crackle. "Oh, right, how silly of me. I get it now. You're having a heaping dose of male guilty conscience, is that it? Wouldn't feel right to bang me after the other Hartford, now would it? What, you think you were in love with Susan and you don't want to wreck the romance by sleeping with her sister? Well, here's a wake-up call: I hate to destroy your macho ego, poor baby, but I have no intention of screwing you. If I'd wanted to get laid I wouldn't *have* to give chase." The titter again. "You think I'm some kind of whore just because I want to talk with you, and I ..."

"It's not that."

"Then what?" she shouted.

The black miasma of rage did a slow crawl up the back of my neck. I brushed my hand over the bandage and my fingers met with a dull heat like a residue of flames. It grew hotter. I rubbed my eyes, knives thrusting up through the other side of my skull. My metaphors were scattered.

"Who do you think you are, coming down on me because I don't come rushing over at your whim? I've got my own life—not that there's too much of it left after the high and hard shredding it's taken since ..." Since when, really? I couldn't remember. "Since I came in contact with your family I've become so bent out of shape I can't see straight. And I'm probably going to get killed because of it, or do some killing, for me and for Susan, so don't pull any of this shit with me, Jordan, I've had enough."

"Christ," she whispered. "What are you talking about?"

Nothing. Nothing. One long, deep breath and most of the armoring calm was back in place. "Nothing," I said. My respect for Susan was boundless. She had done her job so well, chosen her man with such perfect care—her hold on me was as gripping and enticing as my father's. The *Bye* remained on her lips, her smile always turned to me: harsh, sexy, death-defying as she dropped in death.

"Nathaniel?"

The film kept re-winding and playing, re-winding and playing. "I don't know, Jordan. I apologize."

"But ... what ..?"

"I'm sorry."

She didn't say anything for a minute. Then, "You can be a real asshole, Nathaniel."

"This has been told to me before."

"I can believe it."

Maybe a few days in the city, away from the closing walls of my apartment, was what I needed to think the matter through. It would be safer than waiting for the enemy to make his move, giving him a chance to plot his next concerted effort, if there was a plan. There usually is. The forces which had shoved Susan over the edge remained at work, rampant without a clear focus; she'd been killed and consumed, and it still wasn't enough.

"Just tell me something, Jordan," I said. "Why would you ask me?"

"Why?" she said softly, as though she couldn't believe I would ask. "Because you're my friend."

***

We decided she'd pick me up in an hour and a half. During that time I packed three days' worth of clothes and an overnight bag, and brought the dogs over to Carrie's place. She still wasn't home. The spare key was at the bottom of the outside light. I used it and let the dogs inside rather than throwing them in the backyard. Rain flooded the lawn, where four-inch deep pools had formed between trees. The hastily-scrawled note I left on the refrigerator door was littered with lies about doing research for a new book taking place in Greenwich Village. She wouldn't believe it. She'd be pissed, but not very.

I returned to my apartment and was shutting off the engine when Jordan tooled around the corner driving a white Porsche 911, high-powered beams slashing through the torrent.

She pulled up, window open, and said with a bad Brooklyn accent, "Hey buddy, ya need a lift?"

"You can never find a taxi when you need one, but I guess I'll settle for a Porsche."

"You're a man of true mettle."

"Finally, I've met a woman with insight."

Rainbows of the refracted headlights blew outwards across the street, dappling curbs with colors. I got in and had the same trouble with the seatbelts as I'd had inside Harrison's CRX. There was less leg room in the Porsche. The edge of the seat caught my thighs at the worst area of burns, and whenever Jordan made a particularly fast turn I had to bite back a grunt of pain.

"You look uncomfortable," she said. "You okay?"

"Sure." An occasional shriek might tarnish my true mettle. I fiddled with the seat adjustment until I managed to get myself in a bearable position. How could it be no one noticed Susan's wounds? Didn't she grunt with the seatbelts stretched over those criss-crossing patches of welts?

Even with the rain, traffic was light on the Long Island Expressway. We took it in nearly to the Mid-town Tunnel, cut up to the 59th Street Bridge, into Manhattan across town, tearing towards the upper west side. She was much better in city traffic than most people, but then again, she had the car for it—fluidly changing lanes to avoid double-parked taxis, zipping around buses and limousines.

We didn't talk much, but there was no strain in the silence; what we had to say could not easily be said in the confines of a car. Conversation like that needed lots of eye contact and room for hand gestures.

New York City at night.

Almost nobody can remain unaffected, immediately transfused with a portion of its life. Long Island has a wet, horizontal elegance consisting of hundreds of towns and villages, each with its own personality, similar yet idiosyncratic; Manhattan crushes the envelope and compresses people into a nuclear family of millions, with long-standing love and harboring ancient resentments. The excitement is tactile; so is loneliness and boredom. The flow of life moves in a much higher gear. Everybody on top of everybody else. In buildings, subways, crowds, you either progress or you are dragged. Sex and death come faster and easier. Eyes can't help but flit from skyscraper to bodega, scanning gangs of faces in the crosswalks. There is always too much to take at once, above and below.

The moon played hide'n'seek behind the darkly rushing clouds, the immutable skyline cutting a swath across the black backdrop of night. Homeless vets and blind guitar players huddled around the entrance to a bank while a young couple skirted an old woman dragging a pushcart filled with groceries. Lovers were taking in the clubs and the late hour bookstores. Windows of restaurants lit with candles, flashes of silverware, raised glasses of Perrier. There were unsolvable mysteries, traditions upheld, and beauty and hatred which cannot be fully comprehended. You couldn't quite taste the sins or the happiness, but you could smell it all.

"Here we are," she said.

Jordan's apartment was on Central Park West off 72nd.

We got lucky and found a spot in front, and she parked without showing any sign of fear that her car might be stolen, without putting on her car alarm. The building itself was quaint and stylish, with new brick and as much glass as the Hartford home on Dune Road. Shifting sands of Yuppiedom receded into the shadows of Coumbus Avenue.

The doorman was in his early sixties, bald and with a paunch shoved out hard beneath the double row of brass buttons. He greeted Jordan with a broad smile, tip of his cap, and a small bow. He took no notice of me. Jordan and I got into the elevator and she pressed for the tenth floor.

Brushing her wet hair aside and opening her coat, she leaned back against the wall and looked at me. She wore the same winter carnival-type clothing as when visiting me in the hospital—black jeans and a loose red sweater. Her hair trailed over her shoulders, mussed in an attractive fashion.

"Is the apartment yours?" I asked. I'd thought it was a second—or third or fourth—family residence, but Jordan had a certain air of possession about her now.

"Yes. I've had it for about a year or so. Actually, I guess it's less than that. Since March. Seven months. When I'm in Manhattan, I crash. It's a lot easier than driving two and a half hours back to the Hamptons. My parents don't know I've leased it yet. The truth is I haven't had the chance to tell them. It's like that when you see each other as rarely as we have over the past couple years."

"They're out of the country that much?"

"Sure. And when they're home it's only for a week at a time. It's impossible to play a complete catch-up over a five or six month clip."

The elevator doors opened, and I followed her down the hall

to her apartment. The place was huge and carefully decorated with leather couches, furry black and white throw rugs, and an entertainment center with equipment I had no idea about.

"You can put your bag in there," she said, pointing to the guest bedroom. "I haven't been here for a couple of weeks, so it might be a little dusty. We'll open the windows and get some air in here. Would you like a drink?"

"A beer would be fine if you've got one."

I put my satchel and coat away while she fixed herself a drink. I didn't want to open the windows even though they were set with hinge locks so that they'd slide back only six or eight inches. She brought me a bottle of Bud Lite and gestured for me to sit. I did, while she opened the windows to let in a cold breeze and the sound of spattering rain.

Seated beside me, Jordan swirled her scotch and soda, ice cubes tinkling in a slow rhythm. "Would you mind if we didn't talk about it tonight?"

"Okay."

"We will, but not now. Tonight I'd like to learn more about you, and I want to tell you about me. I feel awful you were caught in the middle of what happened with my father. You deserve an explanation. Plus, I'm curious about all I've read in the papers. I want a few answers from you. If you'll give them." She turned her head and took a sip. "But not right now."

Small talk questions came rapidly; we settled into the cushions and chatted about little things of no consequence, working our way towards talking about ourselves. That had its difficulties. The ease with which I'd opened to Susan under the blankets was gone. A part of me knew I was with a different woman and wasn't drunk, and a part of me felt that Susan had stolen what I'd told her, keeping it as blackmail ransom

until I gave her what she wanted; it was impossible to leap a
week backwards, much less a lifetime. I made the effort, anyway. Jordan listened as I spoke of Linda and Randy and the
petting zoo, my miserable royalties, whether I should let
Maurice style my hair, all the etceteras.

I listened and drank and sneaked painkillers I didn't need
while she told me Maurice's efforts were worth every penny of
his two-hundred-dollar-an-hour fee; how she'd had oral surgery when she was seven because she'd knocked out her three
bottom teeth chasing the ice cream man and tripping over the
sprinkler; couldn't stand Mexican, Greek, or Japanese food;
had dropped out of Cornell University after her third semes-
ter; loved Robin Williams and knew somebody who'd been
able to smuggle her into Grand Central Station on the night
they filmed the ballroom dancing commuter scene on the set
of *The Fisher King*.

I knew we couldn't help but force each other; I forced her
to be a substitute for her sister, and she was forcing me to play
out the scene again. It was worth it, though, somehow, for the
time being.

She was shivering, so I shut the windows. It was after one
when the lull in conversation swelled enough for the two of
us to realize we were both tired and should get some sleep. She
said, "I'm glad we got a chance to learn about one another.
Funny how you can come into contact with people several
times and know nothing about them. It was bugging me, you
know? You must've had all kinds of ideas running around
your head when I invited you here, but it's worked out." She
smiled, the dimples etching light parentheses around her
mouth. "You're a nice guy. I'm glad you came."

"I am too," I said, sincerely. "Just don't make any waffles."

"You got it." She drifted down the hall and turned back when she reached her bedroom. "'Night, Nathaniel."

"Good night."

In the guest room, I carefully shed my sweats and got into a pair of gym shorts. I needed a shower, but figured it made more sense to wait until morning when I could wash, put more salve on the burns, and change the bandages. The sheets were satin and the smoothness felt wonderful against my skin. I propped the pillows behind my head and listened to the rain, wondering what Jordan and I would tell each other tomorrow; this respite from insanity would only last until I'd healed enough to complete the hunt, or else fall before another hunter. Standon's face crept up on me, thin and pale and accusing. He'd died in my stead and, at some level, I owed him for that. I swore we'd all be paid accordingly.

Sleep was evasive; when it came on it was so subtle I wasn't aware I'd been asleep until I started awake. I must've dreamed of falling because my whole body snapped back across the mattress. The dust smothered me. I rose to get a drink, looked into the living room and glimpsed the silvery shine of her hair in the moonlight.

Standing by the window, twirling a curl over her fingers, Jordan stared down at the city. She wore a lace nightdress that wasn't particularly practical for October; her nipples were hard and large.

She spun and saw me, and the moment became static—the remainder of the night could go bad, or it could become much finer. When I didn't protest, chastise, whine, holler, or scream, she grinned, and her lips thinned out until the smile remained only in her eyes.

"Uhm," I went. "I thought we said we weren't going to be doing this."

"I think it's time you shut up now."

"Okay."

"Hold me," she said. "Or better yet, I'll hold you."

That would be better. She did, tenderly touching the burns, careful of the bandages. "Is this so wrong?" she breathed against my chest.

She was warm and fit better in my arms than I'd expected anyone would be able to for a long time. Every shred of restraint I had bolted for the nearest life raft. Sweat dripped along my neck. Panting heavily, Jordan licked the salty drops and brought her lips to mine. It felt as if I hadn't been kissed in a lifteime. Perhaps I hadn't been. The straps of her nightgown slid from her shoulders. Murmuring growls of satisfaction we pulled each other closer, down, until we kneeled on the rug. The clothes came off, and I cursed the burns; my bandaged hands were unable to appreciate the entirety of her body.

Her muscles were well defined, stomach slatted, blue veins showing in her breasts. She ran her fingers across my inner thigh and ushered my hands about her. She shuddered and curled herself over my lap, guiding my movements, groaned and gripped my thighs, scratching the burns but not those wounds caused by her sister. Pain sheared through me, adding another level of intensity to the sex; I thought of Susan's knives, the wet instruments laid out beside her on the metal table. I wondered if Jordan's teeth would fit the marks Susan left behind.

"Was it this good with her?" she asked. I pressed my weight on her arms to keep her from hurting me. It was awkward, but tender just the same. Every time the pace quickened, she slowed it without interrupting our motion. Learning her whims was a slow process, gentle in aspects it hadn't been with her sister. All roughness, even the play kind, had been murdered in me for the time being. It was a battle to feel that I wasn't cheating on Susan, or Linda, doing everything as differently as I could. Jordan arched her back and whimpered into my open mouth, saying my name.

Brackman's last words to me spun in the dark like moths, and I thought, *Who am I?*

10

The next morning, while I slept, she went out to Barnes & Noble and bought three copies of my most recent novel. She made me sign them, then read the first fifty pages with a polite enthusiasm that waned when she realized I wasn't going to quiz her on names or hold her responsible for plot.

"I don't go in much for mysteries," she said. "I hope you're not upset."

"Of course not."

"But don't you want your ego stroked?"

"You feed me the best set-up lines for dirty jokes."

"I try hard."

"Keep it up," I said.

"Hey now, that's *my* line."

The banter remained casual. Neither pressed for information, though I wanted to badly; it would take long periods of silent contact before we got into the proper frame of mind to talk about anything that would ruin our momentary gingerbread-house existence. It would crumble. I'd leave it behind. Everyone likes to pretend, acting out adolescent fairy tales.

She changed the dressings and put on more salve, checking the stitches in my scalp; I inspected the burns and found they weren't as bad as they felt, and the blisters were already draining.

The gravity infringed on the coziness. There were less intimate hugs and fondlings. By four in the afternoon the stress had built to such a level that Jordan was anxiously eyeing me, smile thinly affixed, waiting for me to start the talk that would knock our little lover's nest apart stick by stick.

As much as I needed to collect the debts owed, I wanted to make love to her one last time before the bill for this vacation came in. It was nice to dream again. I hesitated to flood her with the incongruous facts of her sister's *after-life*—it would frighten her to discover something continued to prowl in the mist surrounding the Hartfords even after Susan was gone.

Sitting on the couch, legs resting against her thigh, I told Jordan about Susan's commands for rough sex, and my willingness to kill her like that; feeling the puckered scars; Standon and his soft touch with the hairbrush; and the surprise visit from Brackman and his .22. It came off sounding less than it was. Neat and orderly, without much effect. I spoke with an uninvolved voice. Jordan paled, and out of nervous habit she plied the same curl over her fingers. Her color returned after she drank two glasses of wine. She heaved deep sighs and intermittently drawled, "Shee-it," tugging at her bottom lip with her pinky.

"We didn't keep a close watch on each other," she said. "My parents always expected me to act in their stead. I was older and had to keep my baby sister out of trouble. That was the job. I was the mommy figure. If she scraped her knee I put on the band-aid. I made sure she did her homework. On her birthdays, I threw parties. Francis Meachum was in charge of our trust fund, but when the money came in, I was the one who worked it. I think that helped our parents handle some of the guilt because they were absent. 'Jordan is responsible, she'll keep things under control.'"

"Didn't Meachum help at all? The other day he spoke with such authority, like he knew you both so well since you were toddlers."

"No, he didn't help. He's ... not that kind of person."

I supposed not, and Hartford didn't seem like a man who would need to play head games with himself to ease his conscience. He also didn't trust Jordan much.

"Strange as it sounds," she continued, "even though we kind of ran in the same circles, I didn't know where she spent most of her time. She was independent, to the point where she'd take offense if I asked her anything much about what she was doing. You saw what happened when I introduced myself to you at the party. She immediately thought I was grilling and testing the two of you."

I had felt the same way; the implication had certainly been there. "Is that the way she usually acted around you? Defensive?"

"We got along okay, most of the time, but we didn't rush to one another with secrets. On occasion, it got ugly." Jordan couldn't keep all of the resentment out of her voice. "I don't know, Nathaniel. I just don't know anymore."

I didn't either; I didn't even know what I didn't know anymore. I thought she might cry, but she didn't. Only a few quick, dry snuffles. Ever since I'd told her about her sister on the table at the funeral parlor she'd been without real expression, cheeks ashen with shell-shock and wine.

"Tell me about you," she asked, staring off.

"No," I said.

"I want to know."

"No, believe me, you don't."

It was enough difficult conversation. We both knew there would be more tomorrow. She went to the bathroom and got ready for bed, and an hour later when I finished watching the news I crawled in beside her. It was a comfortable scene with an uncomfortable scenario; Jordan close to the wall, hands to her chest, and I didn't feel up to the emotional task of sliding my arms around her and nuzzling my face against her neck. Without Jordan's conscious participation it took more strength for me to keep up the performance than to hold off. I laid flat on my back and stared at the ceiling, listening to her breathing. Playing house was only fun because of its simplicity.

*　*　*

In the morning, she felt like talking. I knew it was almost over and didn't want to let go. The burns on my hands were particularly tender and I swallowed two painkillers with a glass of juice. I got under the blankets and we settled eye to eye, occasionally kissing while we spoke of events, sweeping the shards of Susan's, and our own lives into a single pile.

"It was a nice funeral," she said. "Can you believe I've never been to one before? Even with all the agitation, the funeral home burning down, somehow it came off rather lovely. I thought so, anyway. I don't think my parents could stand waiting another minute ... it was like she was floating around us the whole time, cut adrift. They must've been thinking that not only had they screwed up her life, but her death, too."

I felt the same. Jordan's voice trembled every so often, but she always brought it back to level. "My Dad ordered another parlor to take over and they rushed right into services. Closed casket, of course, top of the line. Must have been three hundred people who showed at the procession. My mother fainted twice. Meachum had to hold her up through it. His shoes didn't go with his suit."

I thought about that. Why couldn't he make enough of an effort to dress properly? Was it because beneath his brusk and haughty exterior he was as smashed by Susan's suicide as everyone else? Had he loved her in his own petty way, even if he couldn't say anything nice about her? Jordan paused and squinted, remembering details.

"My father kept his arms at his sides and didn't move a muscle. The priest was young, younger than me. He gave a nice sermon, or whatever you call it when they speak at the grave."

"Eulogy."

"It was pretty. With a lot of psalms."

I should've been there. One of the mourners could have been the firebug, viewing his handiwork. Setting the fire was stupid, and killing Standon upped the stakes; if he continued to act sloppily, thinking himself indestructible, he might not realize someone could be watching for him. It's how they caught D.B. at the playground.

"Susan was heavily into coke for a while, but she quit it cold. She hung around with John at the time, and he was too much the puritan to ever try any, so she must've given it up for him. He came off as this straight-laced accountant, a brother-daddy-baby kind of boyfriend. Uptight, but still a little crass around the edges, you know? A couple months after they split she started snorting again, a lot more than before."

"You don't know why?"

"Not really. I thought it was because she was sad about John and just wanted to ... you know ... relax. Get back into the scene, have some fun at the clubs. But she dove into it so deep I got a little scared. I mean, she liked the guy okay, but I couldn't imagine her being heartbroken over him. He was more the type to act like that: low self-esteem, hyper-sensitive to a fault. A weenie. Anyway, I told her to calm it down some, but she bit my head off."

"Did you hook her with Sutter? Brackman told me you and Richie spent time together."

"We've known Richie for years. His father and Dad did business with each other. He got a Mercedes for his sixteenth birthday and smashed it up about two weeks later doing triple digits down Deer Park Avenue." Her dimples sprang out as she gave a crinkled grin. "He's ..."

"Actually a pretty nice guy?"

"He's always been good to me. There was a time I thought he'd marry me." Thinking of it made her feel insecure. She placed her arms around my neck and ran her hand through my hair. "But obviously it didn't turn out that way." She pursed her lips and looked away. "He was in love with Susan."

Jordan delivered the line so deadpan that hearing it doubled the shock—a mouthful of the peddler's shiny teeth sinking into Susan's neck wasn't an appealing image. The thought burrowed in and made sense: Susan's natural forwardness and chaotic energy would appeal to a man who needed to envelop that which surrounded him. She would always have something out of his reach, and that would only increase desire. In the long run it would piss him off. Sutter acted with arrogance and contempt. He never loved her, but he enjoyed the chase, and abhorred the fact she ended it so abruptly.

"Brackman said Richie was into other things besides running the club."

She shifted in bed and tried to slough it off. Her hands roamed my chest, stroking hair, twisting me over her fingers. She had suspicions but didn't want to share them. "I don't know."

"Prostitution?" I asked.

"That's ridiculous," she said, knowing it wasn't. "I mean, it's true he fronts some kind of X-rated movie company for a bunch of friends, but who gives a shit? He's never come out and told me, and there's no reason he should have. It's another business. I never asked him. And if you're thinking Richie has something to do with any of this, you're wrong. He would never do anything to hurt her."

Of course he would; anybody would, for the right or wrong reasons. Perhaps she had wanted him to. "You don't sound so sure."

"I am, Nathaniel. You just don't like him, and you're trying to find a patsy." She sat up and was too polite to clamber over me or shove me off the mattress; Jordan slid along the length of satin sheets, hoisted herself over the baseboard like an olympic hopeful. "Now what do you want for breakfast?"

I stayed another day. We screwed happily, sure of ourselves, no longer traipsing about like newlyweds, no need for self-pretense. Discussion had destroyed solemnity. That was okay—we became closer. There was none of the usual post-coital uneasiness that often happens after nights of rousing sex; we were equally adept at watching a movie as massaging each other, laying side by side or on top of each other. Susan's shadow didn't so much darken the game as it added new intrigue. I was bound. I could hear Susan ordering me to return to the hunt. She'd given me time to catch my breath and soothe a few sore muscles. But enough was enough.

By the morning of the fourth day I'd finished the pain-killers; I didn't need the bandages on my legs anymore, and could finally fit into street clothes again. I took the subway to Penn Station and the L.I.R.R. out to the Island.

Back into the past.

***

North Shore breeze carried the clangs of buoy markers over the parking lot. An elderly couple boarded a twenty-foot sail-boat called *Sephora*. Turquoise neon flashed over my Mustang, and I thought about having the car painted. Cats were still crooning, hanging around the kitchen alley door of The Bridge in hopes of nailing a fresh lobster. Distant slaps and stirrings of waves resounded like the arduous strokes of lost swimmers returning home.

I got to the club early, an hour and a half before Zenith Brite's first set. There were new flyers on the front windows, showing her in another pose: onstage and turned to the cam-era, highlighted by the blur of the drummer behind her, ring-lets of hair thrown over one shoulder, head tilted to the left, with an honest, slightly self-deprecating smirk she couldn't quite wipe off her face, as if she was cutting a friend in on a private joke.

There was no line. I was escorted inside by the same woman in net stockings who had seated me last time. Her repertoire remained the same. "Will you be meeting friends or would you like to have a seat at the bar?"

I didn't hand her a fifty. I checked Sutter's table and saw he wasn't in yet. "I think I'll sit at the bar for a while."

"Of course, sir."

The bar was crowded; I sat between a woman sipping a

marguerita and a businessman who smelled like he'd tried to
wash out his ring-around-the-collar in gin. He slumped in his
stool and talked to the bartender, trying yet failing to loosen
his tie. He'd lost the use of his hard consonants. "Twenny-two
years righ down the pipe. Twenny-two years lie they whus
nothin." The bartender refilled the guy's cup of coffee and
urged him to drink it.

I ordered a beer and waited for Sutter or Zenith to show. I
had a brief but earnest affair with the bowl of peanuts in front
of me. The lady with the marguerita started up a short conversation about the rapid demise of the bay fishermen. Soon her
date appeared and they went off to a table near the stage.

If I hadn't been scouting for Zenith I never would have
caught sight of her; through the window of the kitchen door
I saw her eating a salad. The guitarist and bassist spoke ani-
matedly to each other. They were making chord changes, and
she nodded approval. The guitarist plucked a lettuce leaf from
her salad and walked out chewing. While the door was wide
open I met her gaze, smiled, and waved her over. I grinned
when she rolled her eyes, mouth fluctuating between a smile
and those thick, bottom lip worry lines some women get. She
finished her food in two more forkfuls, brushed her hair back
from her cheek, and excused herself from the bassist. I was
always breaking up her conversations.

She made her way over and sat in the empty seat. "Are you
going to bust chops again?"

"It seems to be my calling in life."

"You've got a real hard-on for trouble, don't you?"

"I wouldn't put it in quite those terms, but you're essen-
tially correct."

She sighed. "Well, listen, I don't want to get caught up in

whatever game it is you're playing. Richie's given me the shot I've spent ten years looking for, and I would truly appreciate it if you left right now."

"It's no game, Zenith."

The bartender brought her a diet coke without being asked. Zenith stared at my bandaged hands and frowned. "I can see that. I read about what happened in the papers. I'm really sorry, but I don't know what you want from me."

"I'm not certain, either."

"Well, why are you here?"

To keep pushing. It's not easy making yourself sound intelligent when you're flying on poorly-formed instinct. "I have limited resources. I didn't know Susan Hartford. Richie did. He was close for a time, which might have something to do with why she took her own life." Zenith began to protest, but I cut her off. "I'm not accusing him, but he said he wasn't greatly surprised when she killed herself. He said it with one of his greasy smiles. I'd like to find out more about what he meant by that."

A trio of older men walked up behind Zenith and told her how much they enjoyed her singing in the past, wishing her luck on her performance tonight. She thanked them and, with a flush of humility, signed a page from one of the men's weekly organizers when he asked for an autograph. Zenith turned back and said, "You don't like Richie."

"This is true, but it's not the point."

"You think he has something to do with her death."

"It's a possibility."

"But you're not sure."

"No," I said, "I'm not."

"And you have no proof?"

"I don't."

"Then you are just looking for trouble."

Someone guffawed loudly at the other end of the bar, banging his mug down repeatedly. An instant later Sutter came in through the front doors, closely followed by a redheaded young lady who wasn't much older than sixteen. They sat at his private table and a cocktail waitress brought over a decanter of wine. His entourage surrounded him, led by the Statue of Liberty, spikey hair moussed to sharpened perfection. Liberty looked as if he sincerely considered himself secret service agent material.

"I am looking for answers," I said. "He might have them."

"So why don't you simply talk to Richie instead of being a sarcastic asshole with a chip on your shoulder, trying to stick it to him every chance you get?"

I drank my beer. Zenith glanced at me with a furrowed brow, wondering if I'd take her advice. I wondered, too. I hadn't known what to expect tonight, except the blood taste was thickening. There was something about Sutter I still liked, something I desperately, needfully, hated.

"You're right, Zenith. Let's go talk to him."

She pushed off the bar and waved her hands. "Whoa. It's got nothing to do with me. I've got a show to do in an hour and I really don't need the hassle."

"None of us do."

"Then back the hell off."

I got up. Liberty saw me coming from across the room and whispered in Richie's ear. Sutter smiled even wider at me as I walked up to his table. "Ah, Nathaniel. How nice to see you."

"Always a pleasure, Richie."

This time he reached out and made a show of shaking my hand, noticing the bandages with alarm. "My god, what on earth did you get into?"

"Accidents will happen." Clichés had a way of sticking in my throat.

"Nothing serious, I hope." He felt especially in control; he'd read the papers and decided he had the upper hand. We both understood knowledge is power, and he thought he knew more about me than I did him.

But I'd spent the afternoon in the library, finding out everything I could about the Sutter family and what kind of business it had with the Hartfords. I was hoping to discover some information that might give me an idea on how big a peddler he was, and what else he was into, and whether his father was in on the deal.

I'd gone through five years of microfiche attempting to find a connection. Like Susan and Jordan, Richie made more news in the gossip and society columns than he did the business sections. Some journalist with a taste for smut had caught wind of Sutter buying into Semi-sweet Productions, an XXX film venture. After four hours of searching, the only other article that seemed worth any attention was a sensationalized story of a twenty-year-old porno actress named Gabrielle Haney who'd died of a drug overdose in the middle of an acrobatic sex scene with three men. I backtracked until I had the name of one of her films, then went to the video rental place in the mall and found a copy of the flick. It was a Semi-sweet production.

Richie turned to the waitress. "Sylvia, make sure Mister Follows receives anything he wants, on the house."

"And what can I get you, sir?" she asked.

"Nothing, thanks."

"So," Richie said. "I'm glad to see that you've become something of a regular, Nathaniel. Certainly if nothing else merits a return visit, Zenith's singing does."

"I agree, but there happen to be other things that merit a return visit, as well."

"Yes?"

"I want you to tell me more about Susan. The last time we met you said you believed a person could be a born victim, and that she was one. Why?"

I could feel Sutter's self-centered draw, the pull of the personal vortex circling him; he lifted an eyebrow and his whole face changed, re-casting from roguish to sober. "Didn't we already have this conversation?"

"Up until the part where I said it would have been a waste if she took all your coke out the window with her. Then you got mad and said good-night, and I left."

"What if I ask you to leave now?"

"I will. But I'll come back. And come back again. It'll be a lot less aggravating for you to simply talk to me."

"You may have a point." He shrugged. "Yet it's true I could ban you from my establishment and that would settle the matter once and for all."

"Maybe not," I said.

He shifted in his seat, teeth and ruby tie pin flashing, somewhat interested and rather entertained by my persistence. He told the redheaded girl to go play a song on the jukebox; she went away without a quarrel, two of his entourage splitting off to escort her to the other side of the room. Liberty stayed about five feet behind Sutter's right shoulder.

"I'm not here to take pot-shots or trade quips with you, Richie. I want you to tell me about your relationship with Susan Hartford, and why you were callous to her memory the last time we spoke."

"You have no right to waste my time, Mr. Follows, but I will indulge you. I've read about you in the papers and while I have you here I wish to ask a few questions myself, partic—" He drowned himself out, smiling again, thinking better than to say "particularly about your brother." It was all right, the normal reaction. He whispered for effect. "Tell me why you started the fire at the funeral parlor."

Now he was trying the weak goad. "I didn't."

"Then who did?"

"I don't know."

"Why were you there, Nathaniel?"

Grilling. Cat and mouse. I didn't mind Sutter trying to get information out of me. I was fairly convinced he did not, personally or by his actions, kill Standon. He wasn't subtle enough to be a firebug. Still, Richie was, or contained, a piece of darkness out of Susan's past. I had to get him to shed some light on the recesses where he spent time with her.

I said, "I went to find out about the scars."

"Scars?" He wavered for an instant, his gaze locking steadily on mine—the whirlpool effect grew stronger. Sutter backpedalled without movement, tugging me with him. I knew he was about to lie. He was bad at confrontation, our invisible man, a poor liar by trade. You couldn't see mutilation like that and pretend you didn't. No one gave a genuine performance afterwards.

"Yes," I said. "Blades. Knives."

"I don't know what you're talking about. I cared very much for Susan, more than you'll ever know. If I've acted anything less than distraught over her death it was because our relationship ended on a sour note. To this day I harbor resentments. I am not proud of that fact, but it is the way I feel. I would have given her anything if she'd only asked, but unfortunately, she did not. Yes, I sold or gave her cocaine on occasion, as you so delicately acknowledged when last we met. None of it is any of your business. Susan whined too much, sullen and forever sulking. She was often obnoxious, a tightly-wound girl with a flair for dramatics. She needed to relax. I wanted to help her."

Of course he did. I said, "Is that what you told Gabrielle Haney?"

At the name Richie's eyes widened—it was nice to see him thrown off balance, even if no other muscle in his face moved besides his eyelids—and then, without so much as a hiss, Liberty jumped me from across the table.

Tumbling backwards beneath a two-hundred-and-forty-pound bodybuilder landing on your chest is not an enviable position to find yourself in. He punched me twice in the stomach before I managed to roll free. He got to his knees and slowly stood; the lapel of his coat flapped, and Liberty had a butterfly switchblade in his hand. It was a nice piece of work, with a six-inch blade.

Sutter shouted, "Freddy, no!" Screams erupted, and people in the immediate area hauled ass out of the way; four ladies on the dance floor leaned on the rails, watching safely from that perch, and the redheaded girl ran into Sutter's arms. The other bodyguards didn't know what to do; disarming the situation remained their priority, but Liberty was the aggressor and that threw them. If they rushed me, Liberty would have a clean opportunity to cut out my liver.

He held his blade correctly—underhand, at a slightly downward angle. Slashing in an **X** pattern, he hoped to open my belly, amazingly quick for someone so large. I dodged, but couldn't entirely move clear. The burns slowed me. Wet heat ran down my forearm. I touched my elbow and came away with my fingers colored crimson.

"It's called blood, asshole," he laughed. "Want to see more?"

I smiled and said, "Yes."

Moving in close, I drove the heel of my hand up under his chin as hard as I could. Blood spurted from his mouth, and he took three faltering steps backwards; I followed and chopped his knife hand. I wanted the blade badly. He didn't let go. The burns interfered, but not much now; the bandages were snugly wrapped.

The rage crawled up my head, and I looked for the nearest beer bottle to smash. Liberty closed in. Good. I gripped his wrist with both hands and twisted. He roared as the blade fell. I made a grab and missed, damn it. The knife skittered under Sutter's table. Standing near the bar, arms crossed and holding onto her shoulder, Zenith almost made a grab for it. The redhead jumped too as the knife slid against her shoe, and she didn't know if she should reach down. It would cost her if she did.

I wanted the blade, but let it go. Richie was angry and nervous, but he was also fascinated by the show. Adrenalin surges, and you flinch and wince at the brutality of others, forgetting you're not a participant. I knew, I knew. Sutter reminded me of a Roman emperor watching gladiators fight in the arena, ready to turn his thumb up or down.

Without the knife Liberty wasn't nearly as tough. Like most burly guys, he thought his muscles would do him good even standing ten feet away—he flexed, psyching himself, his nasty sneer a sight. He was proud of all the time he'd put in at the gym, pumping weights and slapping skinny guys across the room, strutting in front of the ladies' aerobics classes. His eyes were lost in the pucker of his squint. He charged forward, swinging a right fist at my temple. I yanked my head back without a quarter inch to spare, hair of his knuckles grazing my cheek; he shouldn't have been that quick. Liberty followed through, spinning completely around. If he'd connected he would have broken my neck.

"I'm gonna tear your fucking head off," he said. "And there's not a damn thing you can do about it."

"I don't suppose you'd consider quitting?"

He growled and blitzed me, punching me twice in the ribs before I could react. I chopped his throat. I chopped again. He gagged and choked. One more time, an inch lower, and he'd be dead. *C'mon, yeahhh.* I shoved a palm into his nose and more blood fountained. It hardly fazed him; Liberty came on. A jab to the jaw made him smile. It wasn't pretty. He roared and dove, his full weight throwing us backwards across another table. On the ground he wildly pummeled my face and chest; my nose ran as I tried to crawl out from under him, the blood taste stronger than before.

Liberty raised his doubled fists over his head, ready to smash my skull. We both knew he could do it. The book said to chop. My brother would have used the knife. I shot my heel out and kicked him square in the balls. He screamed and fell over backwards, nearly at Zenith's feet. She covered her mouth and turned away. He went down and stayed down, clawing at his groin, moaning and gagging.

Richie Sutter drank the remainder of his wine, then refilled his glass.

"Another enjoyable evening, Nathaniel," he said. "Do come back soon, won't you?"

11

My hands were bleeding badly again, I had to soak the crusty bandages off. The gash in my elbow didn't warrant stitches, but cleaning it with hydrogen peroxide wasn't a pocketful of giggles. Next morning, by nine AM, I was oddly exhuberant, as if the fight had hammered a few kinks out of my system. Action reinforces purpose, building as you come to conclusions. I'd been tempted by the blade, and strengthened by resistence.

I jogged halfway to the cemetery and walked the remainder at a fast pace, and spent an hour on my father's grave. The earth was cold and moist, but hard, a layer of frost coating the grass. To our right, someone had left two potted azaleas for *Peter Gerard Leone*, who would forever share my father's point of view. They'd both been dead ten years; I drew my knees up to my chest and wondered who still mourned for Pete after all this time. The azaleas were dying in the freeze.

Fairly far into this maze of Hartford love, sex, and scar tissue, I wasn't much closer to solving the challenge Susan had left me, but I was beginning to believe she helped me drain off other infections. A psychiatrist might consider it a sane pastime to use my father's headstone as a sounding board. I thought about taking the plants home.

No. Pete deserved his azaleas, as well as his viewpoint. There was a gradual incline to the area, copses with evergreens and trees. If you could overlook the dense blocks of mausoleums, statues of the Virgin Mother, and angels with eight foot wing spans, you would think this was merely another grove or picnic grounds. On sunny afternoons there were often as many people here as there were tossing frisbees or lying on blankets at the park. We all revolved.

The day unrolled bleak and gray and fearsome, clouds heavily lined with white and dark roiling shades like a sky full of surf and seaweed. I didn't want to get caught in the storm. I walked one of the paths, but before I was fifty yards outside the cemetery gates, a brown Sedan with a caved-in rear quarter panel suddenly pulled up alongside me, tires squealing. Caution and paranoia have distinct differences; I backed away three steps, ready to duck between the gates if I saw another glimmer of trouble. I could lose anyone in here.

Lieutenant Smithfield threw the engine into neutral and motioned me to get in.

Greasy hamburger bags, breakfast trays, newspapers, and other indescribables littered the passenger side. Smithfield's perfect code of dress didn't match the disrespect he showed his transportation: his three-piece charcoal suit was freshly pressed, and even his overcoat had sharp creases in it. His eyes remained red, and he watched closely as I cleared the seat and sat disdainfully.

"It's the cleaning lady's day off," he said. "If you're going to ask how I knew where to find you, the answer is, I didn't. I was on my way to your place and happened to see you running curbside. I guess you're feeling a whole lot better." He sipped steaming coffee and glanced at the graveyard wall. "Thinking about your future? Looking into buying some real estate?"

"Seems like you're in a bit of a snit today, Lieutenant."

Blinking once, eyes hooded, he looked at me and said, "Tell me that was a joke. Tell me you think I have a sense of humor and want to hear you cracking jokes. Just tell me that."

I didn't say anything.

He positioned his coffee on the seat between his legs and threw the car into gear. "I'll drive to your place." The tires screeched as he accelerated into traffic, he needed new ones badly. We cruised north on the avenue towards my apartment, the sea-sky churning above us, about to crash and drop. It was growing darker by the minute. Smithfield said, "You've been busy lately."

"Idle hands and all that."

"The District Attorney's office got a call from Reginald Sutter this morning. Care to take a guess what he wanted to talk to the DA about?"

"He found a new donut shop?"

That snapped Smithfield's chin up. He sneered and shot me a glance that would have scared most men who hadn't already started to believe that jail might be a safer place than their own homes. "You're a wise ass, Follows, but tell me, please, I've got to know, so just tell me how it is you can laugh knowing your brother was killing neighborhood kids for a couple of years, cutting them up and burying the pieces in your backyard while your father watched and got off on it, too, and you played cowboys and indians over their unmarked graves. We couldn't nail the old man with any proof, but tell me something, Follows, did you watch your brother? Did you know what was happening?"

"No," I said.

"I'll just bet."

Smithfield had nowhere to go. He could either try riling me more or continue in the first vein. He drank his coffee and grimaced, unsure of which tack to follow. A cop, not a social conscience, he started over. "Apparently you stepped on Richie's toes and tore up his nightclub last night. A man like Reginald Sutter tends to take that sort of thing personally. The DA got on the horn and reamed out the Commissioner, who hates Sutter's guts, but in turn handed it down to the Captain, who also hates Sutter, but put it on my plate, anyway. Do you get the picture?"

"Yes," I said.

We approached a yellow light at a major intersection; he gunned the accelerator and ran the red. A large woman snapped forward against her steering wheel and gave him the Italian horns. "Listen, mouth, it doesn't look good when a major businessman grumbles with disappointment. Don't you ever pick on anybody who's not in the highest tax bracket?"

"Watch out for the pothole," I said.

"Don't tell me how to drive." He purposefully hit the pothole, showing off more of the spite lurking within. "Want to recount why you decided to rub your adorable personality up against Richard Sutter?"

"Let me ask you two questions," I said. "Why would Richie go crying to his father over a fist fight in his club, and why would his father throw his weight around unless all was not, as they say, on the up and up?"

"Kicking a guy in the nuts isn't a fist fight." Driving with one hand, he pulled a notebook from his pocket, taking his eyes off the road to page through, negligent of the coffee balanced between his legs. "One Frederic J. Malcomber has the right to press charges."

I snorted. "Which he has no doubt declined to do."

"You think this is funny?"

"No," I answered. "I don't. One Frederic pulled a knife and tried to remove my spleen. He's good with a blade, but not good enough. It wouldn't surprise me if he has been in and out of jail because of it." First spatters of rain splashed the windshield, parading across the glass. "You're not really buying into this?"

"Don't tell me what to buy. A history of violence doesn't even come close to describing you, you know?"

I knew.

Smithfield didn't reach for the wipers. The street flowed and curled. "They've got ten witnesses who saw you attack his son's employee. Ten of Richie's friends would be lying, but that's okay 'cause we'll never have to listen to them, anyway. Charges weren't filed. If they had been, we would have had to question everybody at The Bridge that night and we would have come up with deep shit. I know how to buy it."

I'd told Richie it would be easier if he just talked to me, and I was sure he'd agreed. Who knows what I could have learned if only I hadn't been on edge enough to bring up Gabrielle, and her name hadn't driven Liberty out of his head?

"Do you know anything about a Gabrielle Haney?" I asked.

He frowned and turned on his lights and wipers. "Not offhand. Who is she?"

"An actress in one of Richie's blue movies. She died of a drug overdose a year ago. Mentioning her is what got One Frederic riled, and brought all this heat coming down from

Sutter." We pulled in front of my apartment and double-parked in the street. "Are you getting anywhere with who might have set the fire and killed Standon?"

"Don't question me," he said.

"Okay."

I opened the door to get out and he grabbed me by the collar. Every muscle in my neck and shoulders froze and the cooing rose in my ear. "You mean besides you being our star suspect?"

Uh huh, yeah. "I guess I'm not totally in the clear yet."

Firming his grip, tugging; the cold sweat exploded on my forehead. "If you consider being in the cross-hairs totally clear, then you are." He let me go, finished his coffee, and threw the empty cup into the foot well. "Listen, I don't know what kind of a game you think you're running, but so long as you're playing, I'll be in on it."

I was getting sick of everyone telling me I was playing a game; like a chess match, checking every angle, guarding your pieces. Letting the air out the sides of his mouth, Smithfield sat back and stared at me, and knew I wasn't playing a game. "I think you're more concussed than the doctors gave you credit for."

A truck rolled by and sent a tidal surge of water up over the hood. My fingers worked, fists clenching and unclenching, reaching for a rope that wasn't there.

'Bye.

Susan's voice came as clearly in the car as if she were sitting in the back seat. Gooseflesh broke on the backs of my arms, working the burns. Insane as it sounded—as much as I was becoming obsessed with working backwards—I had not been thinking enough about her ... live Susan. Momentum. I'd picked up so much speed on my own I'd almost left her behind. Conscience is the grand persuader.

"What, Follows?" he asked. "Just what the hell is your concern?"

I said, "Thanks for the lift."

***

The forward charge approach I'd been taking seemed to hinder progress as much as help. There is a time for butting heads and a time for subtlety. Inertia was not an option—movement meant staying alive.

Zenith Brite's phone number wasn't listed in the Suffolk White Pages. She wasn't in the Nassau phone book, either. There were seven Brites in Suffolk; on the fourth attempt I got her mother. It didn't take much doubletalk to convince her I was a producer at Atlantic Records hoping to sign Zenith. She gave me her daughter's unlisted number and the address to her condo. Lies were coming easier.

Not quite noon yet, Zenith was still in bed or just getting up. I knew exactly where her condominium was; I'd been there before, a year ago, when they were in the process of developing the area. The complex nestled between a shopping center and a plush dinner-theater where Linda and I had gone on our third date to see *Shenandoah*. She'd ordered lamb chops extra rare and fudge cake a la mode for dessert. Ridiculous, the things you can never forget.

I stopped at a bagel shop on the way over. The rain pounded without wind, like walking through a car wash. Spotting Zenith's name on the mailbox, I ran the path and pressed her buzzer. No answer. I pressed again; nothing. There was no awning or overhang above her door. I was drenched. I leaned on the buzzer for a full fifteen seconds and figured if she didn't answer I'd try back later.

She came to the door looking like one of the pod people from *Invasion of the Body Snatchers.* Dressed in a white cotton robe, she wore big fuzzy slippers with rabbit faces on them. I smiled. Her chin was drawn into her chest, head tilted down, eyes gazing up from beneath a cascade of disheveled hair. You could see the smoky aura and quirky grin on her lips, even when she wasn't grinning. Haunting ballads still seemed to surround her, songs playing in the background, waiting for center stage.

Yawning, she scratched her ear and pulled a handful of hair aside. "What?" she grumbled. Puffy eyes cracked open a little wider. "Oh Christ, you!"

"I brought bagels," I said, holding up the bag.

"You must be out of your goddamn mind." The whiskers of the rabbits twitched as she shuffled backwards. "What are you doing here? How in the hell did you find me? I ought to call the cops!"

"They've already been called."

"I ought to call them again."

I was beginning to think Frankie the Llama was the only one who liked me anymore. "I didn't know what you might want so I got a bit of everything. There's cream cheese, lox, and some tunafish."

She kept shutting her eyes and shaking her head, went "Uhn," but held out her hand and took the bag. "What time is it?"

"Noon."

Staring past me into the deluge. "God, not rain again. We must've already had ten inches this month. When's it ever going to stop? Why are you pestering me, Nathaniel?"

"I'm not," I said. "I bear gifts."

She bit her lip impatiently. "And just why do you bear

gifts?"

"Can I come in?"

"I don't know."

"Please?"

A wall of rain between us, she stepped out of the doorway, and I followed her. She gnawed her thumb, went to her bathroom, and brought me a towel. It reminded me of Carrie.

Fear made her twist her robe. Zenith was scared, of me or somebody else. In the long run it didn't matter, the effects were the same. "Well, at least you're smart enough not to go back to the club after last night."

"Yes," I said. "I am at least that smart."

"It was a difficult act to follow, let me tell you. Your brawl put everyone in the mood for a Jean Claude Van Damme movie, and instead they got me up there."

"I would have preferred you."

"Yeah, right."

Truth didn't go over well. We walked into the kitchen together, and she pointed to a yellow wicker chair. I sat while she got plates and poured coffee, muttering to herself. She took out butter and a carton of orange juice, casting fervent glances. Clearly, she did not eat, or consequently serve, breakfast much.

Our places set, she grabbed an onion bagel, sliced it open and smothered it with cream cheese. "I can't stand lox. I don't know how anyone can eat it." She finished one half and started to say something else, but changed her mind. Her nose was smeared. "Aren't you eating?"

"No," I said. "Coffee's fine."

She shrugged, a shadow of concern crossing her face. Chewing slowly, she licked her fingers constantly and looked at me, like a dog glaring at another too close to its dish. "I thought

Freddy would hurt you," she whispered. "Really hurt you. I never saw him like that before, and who knew he actually carried a blade?" Everyone did, she wasn't naive. "It was almost as if he was waiting. It frightened me to watch him keep going after you. Where did you learn to fight like that?"

"I read a lot."

Hiding her smile behind her hand, a mouthful of half-swallowed cream cheese is not one of your more delectable sights. I was glad for the grin, anyway. "Are you going to tell me what you want? Last night you said you didn't know, but I guess you've got something solid or you wouldn't be here."

"Nothing solid," I said. "More like gel. Do you know anything about a girl named Gabrielle Haney?"

"No. Why? Who is she?"

"An actress who died a year ago."

"I don't think I've ever heard of her. What was she in?"

"Are you aware that Richie fronts a film company that produces X-rated movies?"

She jutted her chin at me and nodded. "Yes. Do you have a problem with that? A conflict with your Puritan ethic?"

Another good question; people were asking me much better questions than I asked them. There are bad moments you know are coming that you wish you could skip entirely, picking up the remainder much later, after time has passed for the embers to cool.

An intelligent, vivacious woman who would not take kindly to a stranger badmouthing her friend and benefactor, Zenith kept focus. I couldn't think of any other way to breach the subject. Richie had suspected Susan would go in for the swan dive; there had to be a reason he understood her so well. He would tell me sooner or later. I stalked a bad trail.

Zenith ate the other half of her bagel, waiting for an answer. "I can't blunt this question. Do you know if Richie has any dealings with gambling, prostitution or anything else illegal?"

Score zero. Zenith put her bagel down, slowly, each mannerism calculated, as though she might lose control if she did not make a great effort of restraint. Score less than zero. This did not put my heart at ease. She looked at me with such loathing that I could feel the machineries of mistrust cutting me in half, quarters, eighths.

"Christ, you are something else," she said. "You just decide whether a person's guilty and then you keep jumping in their face until the roof caves in, right? Who do you think you are?"

"I haven't decided whether he's guilty or not. That's why I'm asking."

"I don't give a shit why you're asking." Her lips curled into a canine snarl. "Even if I knew, why should I tell you?"

"Because you can't resist my captivating gaze?"

Cause for worry. She leaped up in a flurry of motion—plate flying, coffee spilling—and wheeled away. "Get out of my house."

I grabbed her arm and turned her to me. She struggled violently and I let her go. My own boiling point was absurdly low, anger rising with hers. "You were right last night about my looking for trouble. I am. And it's looking for me, and if I don't find it first I might not make it out of the next fire alive. There's a lot more to it than you know, Zenith."

"More to what? More to you?"

"Yes," I said.

"You're crazy. What are you doing?"

"I'm looking for ..." Breath, beat, unable to put it into

words: I was looking for a lot of lost people, spectres, resolutions, the end of rage, the death of ghosts. "A murderer." Even that came off flat and unaffecting, the melodrama of an insecure boy crying wolf.

"Who? What are you talking about?" Her hair fell back across her face, eyes averted through ringlets. "Susan Hartford committed suicide. What makes you so sure Richie has anything to do with your friend killing herself?"

Because of the way he looked when I mentioned the scars, I thought. I loathed telling Zenith, already dragging her too far into the maze. Backfire, I was not handling the quiet conspiracy properly. Her front teeth hooked over her bottom lip in a pout that would have been unbearably cute if only her eyes weren't filled with such dismay. "I think Susan got into something she couldn't handle. I'm convinced Richie knows what it is, even if he had nothing to do with getting her involved. I think he probably did, though. I need his help."

"What did you do to get Freddy so pissed with you?"

"I mentioned Gabrielle's name. Are you sure you've never heard of her?"

"The actress? Yes." She was confused and tried to clear the air, and I led her back to the table. We sat again. She understood I didn't have a vendetta with Richie, and there was more to the situation than a novelist's imagination. "Believe me, Nathaniel, he's not involved with prostitution or anything else like that. All I know is he owns a house in Dix Hills where they shoot those movies. It belongs to one of the guys who does business with his father. It's not even really his."

Linda lived in Dix Hills. "And?"

"What makes you think there's an 'and'?"

I waited.

She sighed. "Six months ago Richie asked me to be in one of the videos, kinda half-kidding and kinda not. I said no and that was the end of it. I've seen one or two of the movies. They put a lot of money into production values, and they're as heavy on eroticism as they are on the mechanics."

"Where's the house?"

"On Bluejay, I think. I don't know the number but he said it's the only one you can't see from the street, at the top of a long drive. Don't go do anything crazy."

A cat I hadn't seen jumped down from the top of a cabinet and plunked itself opposite me. Patchwork of sand, chocolate, and gold, the cat strode forward with a cautious gait and licked at the discarded tunafish. I hadn't shut the front door firmly enough after entering; it cracked open a few inches, rain coming down, spattering the mailbox, ringing on the metal. Zenith jumped at the sudden noise.

The cat purred, as if comforting hands stroked its back.

***

Bluejay Drive was lined with crooked branches of canopy trees, interlocking like an umbrella of brambles high overhead; in summertime, it must've been picturesque to take a stroll up the road, holding hands with your girl and talking about having babies and the future, early morning dew steaming off the neighborhood lawns. It would still be romantic to walk with her in winter, snow hanging on bushes like frosting on anniversary cakes, discussing Christmas lists and the faces of your little brother as he counted down the days until Santa ate stale cookies left out for him.

But if you were alone in the rainy autumn afternoon it was another circumstance completely—Bluejay Drive was a desolate landscape. All the gardens kept by housewives were shriveled and filled with sticks and sickly plants. A pastiche of colorful dead leaves carpeted the street and sidewalks. Clogged gutters spit back refuse.

I drove the street and spotted a hole punched in the vista, a lot sealed over by elm, oak, and euchalyptus trees backdropping up a short hill. Drainage ditches ran off both sides of a steep gravel driveway. A post-supported glass mailbox showed 1807 in stylized old English script.

I parked at the other end of the block; ditches overflowed into the center of the street, where the water eddied in a tight counter-clockwise swirl. The sewers roared. I checked the post-box hoping to find a letter with a name on it, but only came up with a thick wad of junk mail addressed to RESIDENT and OUR FRIENDS AT ... A redwood fence bordered the property, and a wide gate was held fixed in place by a rope tied through the latch.

No cars in sight. I continued up the path, wet gravel crunching underfoot, the sound of the rain loud on the hill. The drive curved abruptly, and I saw a wrought-iron, modern sculpture sagging in mud. The house was a Tudor with a gabled roof, situated at the top of the long drive, faded into a cluster of woods. Large bay windows faced east. I bypassed the front door, crept onto the back porch, and tried the knob. It wasn't locked, but the door had warped and dropped a half inch in its frame. I had to put my shoulder up against it and nudge hard before it gave.

A broadloom carpet stretched forward, leading into large rooms primarily taken up by mantels and mirrors. Tasteful and demure decor, and the entire place was clean, with the pungent scents of potpourri air freshener thick in the air. A generous amount sat heaped on a tray in the middle of the living room.

No photographs framed on the mantels, no notes on the fridge or dishes in the sink, no decorations, furnishings, or anything adorning the walls, no odds and ends a family would leave around. There was no television. Nothing that added a personal touch or made you think anyone actually lived here; I didn't feel like an intruder because there was no life to intrude upon.

To the left, a staircase rose with dark-grained, wooden railings; I moved upstairs. Bedroom doors were thrown open, exposing art-deco furniture, queen-sized mattresses, and empty bookcases. A third room beckoned at the other end of the narrow hallway, smelling harsher than cherry blossoms and mint, door closed. I pushed it open.

She lay on the bed.

Two video cameras on tripods stood pointed in the nearest corner; several thousand dollars with of sound and lighting equipment rested against the wall and was packed on the shelves. A bathroom reeked of vomit, disinfectant, and peach shampoo. A high-tech entertainment system set up in the huge walk-in closet had been partially disassembled: stereo, CD player, and a Japanese VCR hooked into a twenty-seven inch TV. A computer work station was nearly hidden beneath reams of paper and articles of clothing; a steel cabinet squeezed into the remaining space.

The girl on the four-poster bed lay naked except for a man's unbuttoned blue shirt and a pair of white stockings, one unrolled to mid-calf. Sideways, she had nearly slipped off the sheets, head to the floor, huge breasts hanging over her shoulders. The fine blond hairs wafting in front of her nose should have been a giveaway that she wasn't dead, but I checked anyway. I turned her chin to me and saw it was Gotta-lot Lisa;

her nickname was undeniably true.

Scattered on the nightstand, pink and white pills rested in a quarter-gram mound of coke. Lisa's breathing was frighteningly rapid, and it took me a while to rouse her. Her eyelids fluttered and her eyes circled and wound before they focused on me. "Who're you?" she asked, then, like liquid, slid away, and fell back to sleep.

Cast in a triple-X movie, her provocative factor was off the scale. Pretty, but not especially gorgeous—a bit too plump and sharply featured—she had the qualities of sex beyond beauty. Unknown chemical reactions. Somebody put them to good use, but left her behind.

Lisa sweated and snored, pillows snuggled between her legs. I pulled her back onto the bed and laid her head back. There was no escape from the stale smell of vomit, and no make-up to cover the ugly purple bruises on her knees and thighs. Her girlish innocence was preserved in sleep beneath the lipstick-smeared, stained sheets. I felt ten years older than her because I was.

A cedar wardrobe remained open for inspection, filled with costumes: black and white lace maid outfit complete with cap and apron; blue cop uniform with slitted mini-skirt and a vulgar shaped night-stick; nurse's attire, with the bra split wide for large nipples; a one-piece leather cocoon replete with dangerous studs and dangling chains.

Linda's house was about two miles east of here, close enough to give sharp pangs. I imagined her wearing the cop uniform, hat pulled low, riding me, nightstick on her hips.

I punched up the directory on the hard disk and started going through files, searching for anything that might have a connection to Susan, Sutter, or Hartford. Catalogs and inventories flashed across the screen, movie titles and expenditures, wholesale and retail prices. No mailing lists, no names. With a snarl, I explored farther.

The rages were here; mine and Susan's. The cabinet was locked; I hunted around the desk and found a screwdriver under somebody's gym shorts, jabbed it into the lock and tried to force the top drawer. The screwdriver bent and snapped in half. My heartbeat hammered, migraine suddenly crashing. I grabbed a pair of scissors and did the same thing, prying at the handle and pulling. They bent and broke, too. The hissing thing scampered up my back; my father stood nearby, watching, giving advice. I'd pried the drawer open a couple inches, enough room to grab the edge with my fingers. I planted myself and pulled, kept at it, pulling harder. On the bed, Lisa moaned as if straining with me. With a loud groan of metal, the drawer finally popped out. It was empty.

With the lock broken the others glided open freely. The next two contained nothing. The fourth held screenplays; I was surprised to see there was a large amount of dialog. The last drawer contained five video cassettes, with titles like *You Can Never Go Bone Again* and *The Postman Always Bangs Twice*. They were each labeled a Semi-sweet Production.

I chose tapes at random and fast-forwarded through them; I recognized a cocktail waitress from The Bridge and one of the bouncers, but no one else. Some of the sexual acrobatics had been performed in this bedroom, and a great many filler straight scenes were shot in the house. Zenith had been right; the production values were high. The director and editor played games with light and angles to make each video seem to take place in a different house; particular bric-a-brac like pictures and clocks were moved around various rooms from movie to movie, explaining why none remained downstairs.

In between viewings I checked the window to make sure no one approached. After the last video I turned off the TV, sat back beside Lisa, and wondered what to do next.

When I turned, she was staring at me.

Brow furrowed in puzzlement, her breathing had softened. She lifted her head with effort. "I 'member you." Her voice became surprisingly husky. "You killed Susan." She blinked twice, and then her eyelids found the strength to stay propped at half-mast. "What're you doin' here?" Swallowing thickly, the tip of her tongue peered through her lips. As if she believed she held me at her mercy over an awful secret, Lisa hunkered and grinned with contempt. Her tongue appeared and disappeared like a darting fish. "You come to kill me, too?" She laughed, bitter and malicious gaspings turned into chiding, stilted hiccups. Her index finger flicked out and pointed. "Go on. *In the cellar.*"

12

No longer empty, the house remained unalive—an almost pal-
pable sense of craftmanship weaved through the room as I
retreated. An integral part of a celluloid world, another reality,
this place rose like the dead; heavy on the hardcore, care, and
sensuality, the movies were filmed with more heart and intelligence than you'd think seeing Lisa deserted.

It wasn't Sutter. Susan held no grudge against him. I
couldn't conceive Sutter being foolish enough to allow anything like this to be part of his industry. Not even near being
low key enough, he wouldn't allow himself such disregard for
precaution. I walked down the steps, thinking about how Lisa
was left alone, bruised, wasted like a sacrificial lamb.

Or a Judas Goat.

Thoughts turned. D.B. had started in the cellar, before
moving victims into our backyard. I thought I'd been crazy,
as a child, hearing children, and much later, seeing them. My
father listened to my stories and laughed, though I knew he
was afraid even when he was hurting me.

I gripped the bannister.

The back of my neck filled with claws. No one knew I was coming, unless Zenith told someone after I'd left her. I was slightly nauseated from that cloying potpourri, all the cherry blossoms and vanilla now hanging heavily in the air. It struck a chord and some fragment of memory nearly snapped in place, but not quite. I knew Zenith had been angry, and might have thought me a tad on the deranged side, but I realized she wasn't involved with whatever had driven Susan from the window. We'd had a friendly affinity for one another from the start. But I wasn't going to get her a record contract.

Lisa's witch's giggle had pumped ice water through my veins. I had to find out what was in the cellar.

I had my suspicions.

On the first floor, I opened and closed doors until I found the basement; there was an unused deadbolt at the top. A large set of light switches high on the left, I hit the whole row, illuminating a long stairway of lushly carpeted steps. Paneled walls in bleached-pine and polished brass rails led into a spacious apartment.

My neck creaked when I recognized where I was: a romper room, much different than my brother's had been, but with a similar twist in sensibility; apparatuses of all sorts were on exhibit. A large sectional mirror took up the entire far wall reflecting chairs, swings, a heart-shaped bed, rubber-lined tables, leather straps, handcuffs, and peculiar objects I had no idea about. They looked pleasurable, and painful. I always thought myself imaginative, but I'd missed my education. A device hung that seemed to be made for three people to fit into at once, and, depending on the positioning of your partners, you could wind up with everything from multiple orgasms to a ruptured kidney. There was sharp metal and hooks.

The filler used in the movies lay scattered on the floor: clocks, paperweights, picture frames and smashed glass lay strewn beneath an overturned storage wall unit. Something else caught my attention.

An exposed shoe.

I went over. Behind the collapsed wall unit, face down on the carpet and coiled in his viscera, was John Brackman. His eyes had a faintly amused look, as if he'd fallen for a practical joke and couldn't believe he'd done so. He'd splintered his front teeth thrashing in agony, body contorted like a slug crawling through salt. His glasses rested two feet beyond his reach, one lens cracked, the other missing. Hands failed to hold together the wide rip in his belly, ripples of intestines sluiced out from the wound. His blood had puddled but hadn't completely dried yet; he couldn't have been more than a half hour dead when I'd entered the house.

I'd told him to stay out of it, and he hadn't listened; I supposed I respected him a little more for that, proving his love for Susan one step too closely, so far after the fact. What did he know? What had he learned to bring him here? Perhaps he was more familiar with Sutter's dealings than he'd admitted. Sorrow forced him onto a fixed track. As fractured as he had been after her death, basking before the pedestal raised in her honor, you could see he was glad to die a martyr in the name of love. It was the kind of self-delusion romantics cared about. It explained the content look in his eyes.

"Shit," I whispered, pivoting, expecting to find someone behind me. No one. I leaned against a brace pole and tried to sort it out, but no chorus of angelic hallelujahs played, no blinding revelations struck me. Since there was no official investigation, Brackman's murder would not be tied to Susan Hartford or the fire at the funeral parlor. Three distinct pictures were being painted. The only way to see the connection was to stick your face up against the canvas and risk getting smeared.

Seeing the blood brought back the taste. I wanted to get the hell out. I turned for the stairway.

One Frederic Malcomber, the Statue of Liberty, stood at the top of the steps, head down and feet shuffling out from under him the way bulky men tend to descend stairs. Oblivious to my presence at first, he was both surprised, and glad, to see me.

"You," he growled. Crags of his face writhed, nose wrinkling like an animal's. He looked and sounded like any one of my brother's captured dogs. He hadn't used enough mousse in his hair today and the damp spikes sagged and drooped at all angles. There was a small round bruise on the point of his chin where I'd given him my hardest shot last night—it was not comforting to discover that not only didn't he need to have his jaw wired, but I hadn't even been able to bruise a fair amount. The kick in the nuts had not left him knock-kneed.

Liberty wouldn't be taken so easily again. He was worked up, thinking so many deadly thoughts at once they flashed across his brutish features like teletype: he had to save face, cover up a murder, take revenge, plant another body—the bloodlust poured. He gave a war whoop, rushed down three stairs, leaped, and flew at me.

I got my arms up in time to deflect some of the impact, but the force threw us both across the heart-shaped bed. We bounced and tumbled into the headboard. My skull hit along the stitches and a shower of stars rained. Susan's rage sang. Heat scurried up the wounds of my back, and I felt her fingernails cutting into me again; exotic and heartrending hatemaking ripping through like adrenaline.

My left arm went numb, and the right tingled up through the bone. I prayed it wasn't broken. Liberty got to his feet before me, but he couldn't press the advantage before I put distance between us.

"Where ya gonna go?" he barked, leering. He was right, there was less room to move compared to The Bridge. With the grace of a man who's performed the task many times before, he pulled his butterfly blade from his back pocket and flipped it open. He waved it without any real menace, weaving it through the air like a maestro eliciting music from a symphony. His confidence grew. The smile was smug, dangerous, and self-indulgent.

He hadn't washed the knife thoroughly. A crust of Brackman's blood had dried along the edge. Liberty moved steadily forward. Feeling returned to my arms. I feinted right, hoping he would go for it, and let me spin past the bed, but he was calm and getting smarter, sensing a kill.

I wanted the knife.

Kicking out, I caught him on the ankle. He grimaced and swung in a wide arc, missing my belly, but recovered and slashed again, targeting the same spot. I should have tried to block the motion with my forearm and followed through to break a rib, but with all that muscle guarding his bones, if I missed he would have a clear opening to carve my face. He was in no hurry. Neither was I, really. I backpedaled and sucked in my stomach as he drove at me again, twisting to keep balance. I caromed off one of the devices I'd never seen before and crashed into a red-leather table.

He laughed, once, and stabbed down at my chest. It would have been a nice killing stroke, if I'd been afraid of the knife.

I caught his wrist with both hands, dropped my shoulder, and yanked. Liberty didn't go sprawling behind me, but it forced him to drop the blade; he stumbled and recovered fast, spun and punched me below the ear, then did the same on the opposite side. The nerve masses there jangled to life, and it felt like my whole face had been driven through with Susan's wet instruments. She said something I couldn't quite hear. The children gathered.

Liberty jabbed again, lower on the hinge of my jaw, and blood ran from my split lip. He tried to grab me around the waist. I hit him twice, turning and putting my shoulder into it, whirled and brought an elbow back into his stomach. He was in extremely good shape and didn't go down, but he moved off with a loud grunt. He could afford to take a breather, assured I had no way to escape. The knife had dropped under the sex swing built for three. We were equidistant from it.

"You're gonna die this time," he said.

"No. You are."

On the ground beside me, Brackman stared on with his amused look, rigid fingers unable to suture the gaping hole that had been his abdomen.

"Why did you kill him?" I asked.

Moving in tight circles, Liberty hoped to divert my attention. His biceps bulged, contours of his hard muscles like chiseled stone. He would stoop for the knife. I would roll. We'd see who managed it.

"He was a nosy prick, just like you. He started asking questions and pulled a gun on me." A grotesque smile sheared his face. "Fuck him and fuck you. He's lucky he died pretty quick. I should've tied his guts in a knot and strangled him with them." Liberty's cheeks flushed, as if the thought excited him and he couldn't wait to try it out on somebody. He barked once more. "You know what the funny thing is? His piece wasn't even loaded."

I'd taken the bullets out of it at my place four days ago and he'd put the them in his pocket. He never bothered to reload.

"What happened to Gabrielle Haney?"

"You'll never know."

"Of course I will."

In one motion he whirled, lifted the storage unit, and heaved it at me. He made hurling a hundred pound piece of furniture look easy. It was a bad throw for both of us; he missed but I couldn't roll to the knife. I dodged the toppling shelves, yet he was now a step closer to his blade. My ears still rang. He enjoyed himself, cutting his initials in men, fulfilling his lot in life, putting an end to nosy pricks. I wondered what One Frederic had buried in his backyard, and if his father had watched him.

The tip of his tongue slid out the corner of his mouth as he grinned, eyes holding no more depth than shadow. He would lynch me with my own entrails if he could. The knife would be mine.

My head pounded and Brackman's blood was everywhere, and something very much like a levee broke inside my chest, an icy clamp suddenly released, and Susan's voice became clearer, and I'd give up anything so long as I could be with her again, and not fail this time.

I vaulted the table and came down on Liberty's back as he bent to grab his blade. He went floundering forward, with me holding on like a crazy kid playing piggy-back, and together we went crashing into the sectional mirror. Shattered glass rained over us.

I fell off him and held his knife arm to the side, brought the heel of my hand up under his chin the same way I had last night; he was leaning back and I barely connected a glancing shot. He tried to knee me in the groin, but I shifted and took the brunt on my upper thigh; it still hurt a lot. Glass crunched beneath our feet. Turning, he threw a shoulder into my chest, and gave me a roundhouse with his free hand. Blood ran over my chin.

Liberty had the advantage as we wrestled, but he didn't know what to do with it. He badly wanted to cut me, and kept fighting for that rather than using those massive arms to crush me. I maneuvered behind him, locked his left arm and pulled. He let out a howl and planted his weight and twisted, hoping to force his fist into my throat; it was the wrong thing to do. Breaking his arm was a lot simpler as he braced himself out of position, no upper body leverage to throw me off. The pop was sickeningly loud.

He screamed. Last night I'd cringed a little when I'd nailed him in the balls, feeling some empathy, if not remorse. Now there was only the miasma of rage crawling over my shoulders and into my chest. He paled. Tears and large beads of sweat mingled and dripped down his face. I let him cry and tremble, holding the busted bone, tugging him onto his side while he curled into a fetal position.

When he grew accustomed to the pain, I dragged him up until our noses were an inch apart.

"Why did you kill him?"

"Fuck you," he snarled between groans, spraying pink spittle.

"Tell me."

"Fuck you."

"Tell me or it's going to hurt a whole lot worse."

"Eat me."

I sighed. "At first I thought Gabrielle might've been your girlfriend, and she died partying on one of your movies. Now I know you for what you are. You flipped when I mentioned her because you killed her too, didn't you? Why?" The voice didn't sound like my own anymore; it bordered on the irrationally, murderously calm. "Answer me."

"You should've burned," he said weakly.

"You set the fire and killed Standon, too."

"I should've cut your heart out."

"You couldn't," I said. "Who do you work for?" I waited. The knife was near. "Tell me."

"Fuck ..." he eked out, and looked at his arm and saw the unnatural bend to it. He lifted his other hand as if to press shattered bone, wanting to put it back in the usual place.

"Last chance," I said.

"Fuck ..."

"Okay, you're dead."

I reached for the knife, but, as I touched it, one of the shards of mirror seemed more useable. I picked it up, feeling it's capability to slice into my hand. It didn't. I could cut Liberty's face off in two minutes with the glass. He was the one—he'd been there for my first meeting with Sutter, when we'd discussed born victims and victors. Which was Liberty? It didn't fit together, any more than I did when looking into the shard of mirror. *Who are you?* I didn't know.

I would never hurt you," he said, taking me in his hand, and hurting me.

"Jesus."

My father must have had reasons to do what he did. I had

my own. I turned Liberty over until I got a good look at his throat. I dropped the shard and smashed him in the nose. He was already unconscious.

I stood up ready to scream, not knowing for whom, or for what. Nothing came. I stumbled over him towards the stairs and dropped to my knees.

And saw the tapes.

Two more videos were lying on the floor. They'd fallen from their place in the medicine cabinet-like niche behind the third section of the mirror we'd smashed during the fight. It was probably not so secretive a hiding spot as it seemed, but not much would surprise me.

More porn? Snuff films? Evidence?

The acrid stink of blood added to the headache, and Gene Krupa played Drum Boogie behind my eyes. Liberty was too heavy for me to carry up the stairs, and I wasn't certain if I should tie him or not. His breathing became ragged, lips going blue from being so contorted. I dragged him over to the table with the fur-lined handcuffs and cuffed his good hand. I wanted to get him to Smithfield as quickly as possible, but Dix Hills was an hour away from Southhampton and the Lieutenant's jurisdiction. That meant bringing other cops into Susan's tapestry.

I took the videos, climbed the stairs, and threw the deadbolt on the door. One Frederic Malcomber wasn't going anywhere. I hunted through the kitchen and living room searching for a telephone, but there was only a portable phone unit with no receiver.

The police weren't going to like my story. On the second floor, I thought of watching the tapes immediately, but I needed to leave the house to call the cops. The idea of leaving Brackman's

corpse in the basement for longer than necessary didn't appeal
to me. I had no choice. Lisa was still out of it on the bed, gently
snoring in a near soundless manner, reminding me of when
Susan fell asleep in my arms on the beach. There was no sense
in leaving her for the cops; I didn't know what kind of a situation she was in, but for all I knew being found like this might
ruin her life. I got her dressed and semi-coherent.

She followed me like a puppy, staggering out of the house
and down the driveway, bottom twitching. The rain didn't do
anything to snap her out of her daze. "Where we goin'?" she
asked.

"Home," I said.

"I don't wanna go home."

"Where do you want to go?"

Lisa thought about it. "Home."

She had no purse or identification on her. "Do you live
nearby?"

With big, bobbing nods, she said, "Yeah."

"You show me."

"'Kay."

Walking to my car, she slid on wet leaves and hurtled
towards the gate post. I caught her and kept an arm around
her until we reached the Mustang. It took a while to get the
address out of her—her place was in Linda's neighborhood.
When we pulled up I saw even the architecture of her house
was the same.

If she lived with her parents they weren't home. At the
front door I realized she had no way to let herself in. Either she
was used to such returns or she'd thought ahead, because she
kept a key under one of the seashells in the garden at the side of
the stoop. We entered together, and she sank onto the couch. I

called Smithfield's precinct first because it would take him time
to get out to Dix Hills, assuming he came at all. Then I called
the local cops and gave them an overview of what had happened at the house on Bluejay Drive; they asked question after
question. I explained I'd meet them there and hung up.

I turned Lisa on her side and threw a crocheted blanket
over her. The harshness of the world fled her face as she slept:
soft, unlined, without much wear or damage. If only we could
remain so untouched while conscious.

***

I met the blue and whites pulling up on Bluejay Drive. Sirens
and flashing lights tore hell out of the silent, overcast landscape. People came out onto their lawns and crowded the
sidewalks. Four police officers carefully appraised me without
introduction, questioning further. I showed them the basement door and told how One Frederic Malcomber and I had
brawled, and that he'd admitted killing John Brackman and
Andrew Standon and setting the fire that had destroyed White's
Funeral parlor. They didn't look as if they believed me.

A lady officer with hair that refused to stay under her hat
asked to take my statement while another cop searched the
second floor. The remaining two went to the cellar.

She flipped through her notebook to an empty page and
gestured for me to start talking, but there was no way to know
where the beginning was anymore. I wasn't sure how far back
to go. I didn't want to involve Zenith Brite. I admitted I'd met
Brackman at Susan Hartford's birthday party, and went into
detail about the fight with Malcomber at The Bridge. The
bullshit cover story I set up to explain why I'd been at this
house in the first place never came up; they never asked.

I actually hoped Smithfield would show up quickly; I'd rather deal with a familiar cop's glaring heat than an unfamiliar one's. The lady looked the way I thought an officer of the law should: a no-nonsense sharpness to her attitude, always on guard, intent on justice. It's how I described them in my novels. Jacob Browning would've been able to wheedle a smile out of her, but life wasn't going to reflect art. She asked more questions and I answered. Only a few minutes passed before the two officers from the basement came upstairs and pointed their billy clubs at me.

"There are two dead men down there."

The lady cop stepped away from me and turned so that the three of them faced me in a line.

"What?" I said.

Liberty had been rasping badly, and I was no doctor. The officer who'd been searching the house returned and drew his club when he saw everyone else standing around with theirs drawn, staring at me.

"I didn't lie to you," I said.

"Let's check it out. Bring him. I want to hear what he has to say."

One of the cops drew his gun and stayed in the kitchen while the rest of us went to the basement. Liberty was dead all right, still cuffed to the table where I'd left him, wrist chafed and lacerated where he'd tried to wrench loose. I wouldn't have to salve my conscience: there was a quarter-sized hole in his head directly over his left eyebrow, trickling blood. Brackman's body had been moved to a different position, rolled onto its back as though managing a monumental spurt of exertion hours after he died. His .22 lay near his viscera-covered hand. An officer touched Liberty and trapped gas bubbled from his throat.

"Somebody came here and murdered him while I was out calling you people."

They almost laughed in my face. If I'd written the line for a character in these same circumstances, I would've had the cops laugh in his face. We went back upstairs. I related the story from the beginning, leaving out any mention of Lisa and the two tapes I now had under the front seat of my car—editing myself was becoming a real bitch. The cops kept conferring, whispering, unaware of how loud they are. They were getting ready to bring me to the station when Smithfield showed up.

He didn't look or talk directly to me. The officers led him to the basement and he came back up shaking his head, rubbing his hand across his upper lip. He spoke quietly to the lady cop and took her notebook, then read my statement back to me, emphasizing One Frederic Malcomber's name, dragging the syllables out. "I talked to you seven goddamn hours ago, Follows. How did you manage to wind up hip-deep in dead men since then?"

Jacob Browning's snappy answers eluded me.

Smithfield sighed. "Don't try to be witty. You look like you're about to say something wise ass. I've had heartburn since I've met you, and when you try to get witty my ulcer acts up." He snapped the notebook shut. "You broke that big son of a bitch's arm?"

"Yes."

He leaned in closer to me, mouth to my ear. "You shot him."

"No."

He shrugged. "This guy, Brackman, had a gun?"

"Yes, but Malcomber said it was unloaded. Brackman was dead at least an hour before Malcomber. Whoever killed Malcomber turned Brackman's corpse over, found the bullets, loaded the gun, and then shot Malcomber."

He stared at me, eyes and voice perfectly level. "He almost tore his own hand off trying to get away, knowing what was coming."

"Malcomber left too wide a trail behind him," I said.

"You sure do know a lot about how a killer thinks, Follows."

I did. I tried not to sound inane but didn't quite pull it off. "I can see from other perspectives."

He nodded with his usual suspicious glare, and I thought he might comment further on his Vietnam sniper experiences. Other police arrived in the meantime, and with them was a photographer and the EMTs.

Smithfield said, "What did Brackman do?"

"Do?"

"What was he employed as?"

"An accountant."

"Too bad he wasn't a writer, too. Then maybe he would've been as brilliant as you, and the poor bastard wouldn't be dead."

"Maybe."

I told him this was the place where Semi-sweet Productions made their blue movies. "Have you checked into that? What have you got on Gabrielle Haney?"

"I told you not to question me," he said.

I swallowed. "I'm sorry." Smithfield motioned me towards the dining room. I turned and said, "I think ..." Some sentences shouldn't be finished.

His hands were those of a man who had toiled hard from an early age and would never stop. I could tell that when he threw me up against the wall and pinned my shoulders.

"Now listen to me very carefully, you little turd," he said. "I don't work for you." It took a colossal effort to keep himself from hitting me. "You might think you're off the hook and that you and me are bosom buddies, but you'd be as far off base as you could be. You are a mouth, and I think you're a sick puppy too, like your kiddie-killing brother, and your evil old man. I hate mouths, and I hate messes like this shit here even more. I'm going to say it in plain English one more time, in case you've forgotten: if you are fucking with me I'll toss you in a cage with the other animals and leave you there until you die. I might do it just to make sure, understand? Just to make sure you ain't got your family's bad blood, which I think you do. A smart guy like you should be able to understand that, right?"

I understood.

***

The dirt had caught up with me, and was clinging.

I needed, I thought, to feel clean and human again, and to have someone who cared about me hold me in her arms. I wasn't sure if there was anyone who fit that description anymore. Driving rain on the windshield accurately depicted these last weeks, one scene flowing into another. Torrential, cascading, gray.

I drove to Linda's.

Three blocks to her house I became aware of the tingling sense of expectation I always got when going to see her; it was nice to know some things hadn't changed. Headlights flared in the murky gloom of an October evening, illuminating the flight of leaves driven from branches in the downpour. I'd more or less forgotten that tomorrow was the thirty-first. I pulled up and saw her windows were covered with Halloween cut-outs she and Randy had made from fabrics: cackling witches on broomsticks, spitting black cats with arched backs. Indian corn decorated the mail box. A pumpkin the size of Cinderella's carriage sat on the stoop, carved into a visage with fearsome eyes and a crooked, grinning mouth. A six-foot skeleton danced on the door.

Jack's car was in the driveway.

There was still no chorus of angelic hallelujahs, but this time, I was struck with a blinding revelation. The reason for that expression on Jack's face the day he visited me in the hospital, the look of shame, became self-evident. His reproach when he thought I had left her, and his phone call and constant reaffirmation that Linda was a special lady, took on new and urgent meanings.

Other curious events made sense and no longer seemed random: Carrie waiting for me at my apartment, silence and preoccupation and neediness. The obvious static between her and Jack, and the way she cried in the hospital. I recalled thinking at the time she had wept for more than my burns, that she shed tears for Jack, as well. I had mistakenly believed it was because she'd imagined a day when he would be killed in the line of duty. Presumptious of me, thinking that rather than something as close to the bone as a broken heart. Love lost was at least as critical a condition.

Laughter caught in my throat, coming out, "Humph."

I had taken his girl and he'd taken mine, but where I'd had sex, he'd gained family. There was a time he would have thought me better off, but we both knew the truth now. It had happened before between other friends and other girls, but you're never ready for it. Especially at the moment when you return to her in the bad hours, empty of everything except nerves and memories and loneliness, hoping to rekindle some of the passion you once had, and find another man there.

And my friend would be right if he ever chose to tell me that he and Linda were adults and could make their own choices, that I was no innocent because I hadn't waited even twenty-four hours before I'd been with another woman. There are times when sitting in your car listening to the busted fan of the heater is as bad as hearing yourself scream.

The jack-o'-lantern grinned, daring me to knock.

Time flew circles. I don't know how long I remained laughing at the irony of love lost and re-lost before I noticed Carrie's car up on the opposite side of the street, staking Linda's house out. I drove on and double-parked next to her, left my car running, and got in beside her.

The strain had taken its toll. The flesh around her eyes was dark and dull, the slant of her mouth already causing creases. Her jaw had been set firm as a boxer's. She'd had her fill of crying and wouldn't be able to call up any tears for a long time to come—at least another half hour. And then, when she didn't suspect it, she'd break down like a marionette with the strings clipped. I could see it. She saw it in me, too.

There seemed to be no safe place on earth, no faith or ideal we could stand on that wouldn't eventually crumble and slide, because of us or in spite of us. From the water, the horizon looked the same, no matter in which direction we floundered.

"Now you know," she said.

"Now I know."

"When did you figure it out?"

"Now."

Stilted and malicious chuckles. "I tried to tell you a couple of weeks ago, but I figured you would've thought it was all in my imagination. And then again the other day, but you had other things on your mind."

"My fault," I said. "Sorry."

"My fault, too. I could've talked to you instead of screwing with you, if I'd had the courage."

"I just wasn't listening."

She shrugged. "And I was always worried they didn't like each other, can you believe it? Silly me."

We would feed into each other's anger if we remained here much longer—conspirators spying on conspirators, giving up rages all over again. There had been enough. I wanted to unplug myself from the ache before it diverted me onto even more loathsome avenues. I still had work to do.

Carrie nodded wearily. "I'm going to sit here until he comes out. I want to see his face. I want to see her face, when she hugs him one last time at the door before he goes. I want them to know they aren't fooling me."

"Don't stay."

She humphed. "No, I should be at home feeding your damn dogs, right? I should be cleaning their shit up out of my back yard, right? You, the big advice-giver."

"You're only making it worse, Carrie. Go. Anywhere but here."

Her head swayed slightly back and forth with the motion of the wipers. "I thought the son of a bitch loved me. I thought she was my best friend. Screwing is one thing. It's bad enough. He's screwed other girls plenty of times. I've caught him before. But this ... this, god, this, I know, they'll say this is love."

"Maybe it is," I said.

"Go fuck yourself."

"This isn't doing anyone any good."

"I don't want to do good," she said, keeping her gaze pinned to the house. "I want to see his face."

I didn't. I had visions of him walking out the door, turning back and giving my girl one last kiss, smooching the way lovers do after a cold autumn's day inside, warm and contented beneath thick blankets. He'd be gawky from laughter and she'd be smiling serenly, eyes lit with affection. I wondered if it had been going on since before that final night with Linda, and if Jack's attentions hadn't added to the fall, or caused it. Or if I drove her to him. Or Carrie drove him to her. I wanted to smash the pumpkin. Halloween was already a dead season.

"Don't stay." I got out of her car and back into my Mustang.

Carrie remained like a loyal soldier guarding a fort already lost.

***

No foreplay, no meaningless waste of time on words. Nowhere left to go but the basement. The girl on the first tape was in her early twenties, with elfin features, red hair, covered with caramel-colored freckles. The man in the ridiculous leather mask said virtually nothing that was not a direct order, and she obeyed his commands.

At one point, while she twisted wildly as he clamped her ankles to her wrists, he called her "Ellie." He used burning candles and paddles and performed other sadistic acts on her, the kind that don't leave permanent physical marks. She was released from one position and firmly bound and gagged into another, switching masked partners as she was covered with feces and urine.

She took it all with the grace of a trained masochist, crying out only when her endurance was at an end.

I drank rum until a wall of cotton surrounded me and I was inured enough to put the next tape in, knowing what would be on it. Susan was younger, her hair swept in a different hairstyle I didn't prefer. There should have been time, I thought—time for her and me. At least as long as Jack would have with Linda. Trust. If only we had been able to forget the past long enough to trust, if only I hadn't been my father's son. I couldn't shrug off the feeling of unfairness, as though the fates of Susan and I had just missed each other. It had been close. She should've given me a chance. And perhaps I could have earned her love.

I watched as she took a razor blade and dragged it across her chest, back and forth, digging.

Staring into the camera.

At me.

13

One of the worst sensations is having a nightmare and realizing you are asleep, head rattling in darkness with the thought, *it's only a dream*, until the moment you discover it's not.

Fact mingles with fiction in such a state—and this time I was a step quicker and managed to avoid Fatter Ernie and catch hold of her ankle. She stared up at me, smiling, relieved and grateful I had finally done my duty. There were sounds like the clinking of the front door knob turning. Distorted faces came at me with knives and torches.

My eyes snapped open. I listened for the dogs, forgetting they were at Carrie's. The dream receded. Something else ticked at the edge of my mind. The hangover gathered speed, and I was still a little high from the rum. The moon unraveled through the top of the curtains when Sutter and four of his boys broke in.

Quickly and quietly. The lamp snapped on and two bruisers hauled me off the mattress, bent my arms behind my back, and forced me to my knees. Richie stood in the middle of the room, flanked by more Neanderthals. Cavemen who wore wrap-around mirrored shades and Pierre Cardin suits, gloved fists clenched over belt buckles. They looked bored, the kind of bored not even a serious beating would perk them out of. Sutter said nothing.

On one level, he hardly seemed to notice me. On another, he made it clear that whatever borrowed time I'd taken from him was at an end. *Careless, so goddamn careless.* My skin went clammy as nervous sweat slithered. I had insulted Richie, underestimated him—and he wanted me to take a few minutes to reflect on that.

Glancing around the room, he walked to the bookcase, and checked through philosophy and history titles. Some prompted him to grunts of appraisal. He opened the Bible, found and counted the two hundred and change I keep stashed there, and put the cash back. Silently as one of the cats stalking the alley behind his club, he stepped out of my peripheral vision as he continued across the room.

I heard him going through drawers behind me, shuffling papers, tossing clothes. Photo albums opened, were flipped through, and clapped shut. When he got to the folder stuffed with rejection slips, he chuckled. None of Richie's men moved an inch. My weight was on my knees and the shin splints were killing me.

Richie stooped close behind and spoke in my ear. "Saint Augustine is brilliant, but I've found him a tad too dry."

"Me too," I murmured.

Both thugs yanked my arms up a notch and I would have cried out if one of them hadn't slapped his catcher's mitt-sized hand over my mouth.

I shifted my weight and tugged forward as if relaxing. I needed three more inches, just enough room to snap my arm back. The positioning was clear, the snap of our bones evident. I would give up a busted wrist for a chop at a throat, a chance to wheel for the kitchen drawer.

But there was no real need to think along those lines: Richie was a talker, and he'd come to speak on his terms. That was acceptable. I'd sweat it out so long as I got answers.

"I'm particularly fond of the quote, 'Necessity knows no law.' It's something my father taught me early on, Nathaniel. Perhaps your own dear old dad taught you the same." He came forward and fit back in between cavemen, hands clasped as theirs were, staring down at me. I thought we might make a good Vaudeville act. "What are your feelings about the law? From your actions I'd say you have no compunction to break it when you feel the need to do so—and as of late you've felt it quite often where my business is concerned. I don't appreciate that. You've been having a bit of fun at my expense, haven't you?" True to form, he actually expected an answer. He gestured for the thug to let me speak. "Haven't you?"

The bear paw unclamped from my mouth. "No, Richie, I haven't."

"No, I can see how you might not." His thick lips eased into that peddler's slick, shining smile. "Certainly not at the moment."

Even from my position, I could manage to kick in his teeth. It would be incredibly fulfilling. The pain in my wrenched shoulders was quickly becoming unbearable. For whatever weird reason, I wondered whether Jack spent the night at Linda's, and what they would tell Randy when he found them together in the morning, and whether Carrie would still be waiting. It was difficult to control my voice. "What do you want?"

"An explanation, of course." He enunciated his words with

extreme care. "You trespassed on my property, delved into private business files, destroyed personal belongings, and left two men dead. All in order to disrupt my life." The tone he used didn't quite lower the temperature of the apartment, but he was trying. He went to one knee before me. "Consider it disrupted, Nathaniel."

"I just wanted to talk, Richie. You lied about Susan's scars."

Sutter pursed his lips. "All right, the truth then. We'll have it. Yes, I did lie, more from astonishment than anything. I wasn't expecting you to know about her. I was her lover for a time. It shocked me that you should be aware of her secret. It was one only an act of intimacy could reveal."

Something else, somewhere else, was coming apart, about to give. "It couldn't have been much of a secret if she sliced herself up on video for you."

The bruisers tried to hitch my wrists up until they touched my nape, but the rage kept them hard and low. *Oh yeah.* My shoulders cracked. This was tiring.

Richie became dead serious. "What are you talking about?" He told them to loosen their hold. "Answer me."

"You filmed her."

"Filmed Susan?" he said, confused. My stomach dropped. "Ridiculous."

"For your movies."

"You're talking nonsense."

As much as I hated him, I realized Richie wasn't acting out a role. The invisible man wasn't a persona to have on a stage. Malcomber had been stupid and sloppy, but he'd dispatched Standon and Brackman with cold efficiency. No style, verve, or wit. Sutter was a main player, but perhaps he had too much class for real bloodletting.

Now, if only he didn't try to kill me and wreck that theory.

Vague hunches spun. Love, abuse, guilt. Trust. More sections of Susan's shattered life slid into place, and when some of the pieces didn't fit I jammed them in sideways, seeking the correct approach, the right access.

"You asked me why I'd been at the funeral parlor. I told you it was to find out more about the scars. The mortician said they had been self-inflicted. He was later murdered. Now let me up."

Sutter inspected me from top to bottom—knotted veins, stink of liquor, sweaty hair dropping over my forehead, and finally my eyes. Kicking in his teeth was still an option.

"Let him up," he said.

The caveman brigade obeyed and kindly helped me to stand, with a show of interest in my well-being. Richie said, "Convince me why I shouldn't allow my men to break your extremities."

"First tell me about Gabrielle Haney."

He didn't like me taking the offense, but since he had nine hundred pounds of brute strength backing him up he didn't bother to quibble. "She was a childhood acquaintance of mine who eventually became an actress in several adult videos. She accidentally overdosed on barbiturates and died last year."

"Movies from your production company."

"I am partial owner, yes."

"How did you meet her?"

"Just as I said, we met as children. Her father did occasional business with mine."

"Why did Malcomber attack me when I mentioned her name?"

"I don't know, but I didn't mind, and I tire of your

questions. Don't press your good fortune. Tell me what I want to hear."

I massaged aching muscles, unable to decide what I felt; the rage would've been much more bitter if I wasn't so damned sure I had forced our meeting to occur this way. The initiative sometimes backfires.

Except for the conversation with Zenith, I repeated the story from the beginning, just as I had for the police. No emotion showed through the mirrored glasses of any of the four thugs as I explained what had gone on in that house. Richie had feelings, but he covered them well. When I got to the part about discovering Lisa abandoned and bruised, he sucked wind. The rest of it made him frown and fiddle with his tie, as though he felt he was losing control of his appearance. Because his features could alter considerably with one facial tic, it was almost impossible for him to remain a blank. Mentioning the videotapes destroyed his illustrious cool. Maybe he really had once loved Susan. At least as much as Brackman.

"What were you to her?" he asked. "Why have you come this far?"

Like everything else I had with Susan Hartford, I had only a thread of the whole.

"I was her friend."

"Let me see those tapes, damn you."

They were on top of the VCR. The first slipped into the machine with a loud *thunk*. Richie stood in front of the television, rocking on the balls of his feet, holding the remote control before him like a dagger. He got through a minute and a half of Gabrielle and then put in the second tape. He lasted fifteen seconds.

The look on his face wasn't that of a man who is watching

a loved one defiling herself—instead, his expression was of
somebody who is confronted with hard evidence that all that
pain had not only gone on under his nose, but was financed
with his money.

"Frederic," he whispered, "was employed in several capaci-
ties. One being that he supervised ... Semi-sweet Productions."
The name was so absurd even he had difficulty saying it.

"I figured out that much going through the files. But
somewhere along the line Malcomber went into business for
himself, using props and equipment from the company. Did
he know Susan and Gabrielle well enough to ..." No words
came. I tried.

"Coerce them into this *enterprise*? No, he didn't. I almost
can't believe anyone could have compelled them to do that,
certainly not the likes of him. It was an outpouring of some
sort." He glared at his men, checking for information. They
moved themselves as if gray matter actually did exist at the
top of their spines: all four shook their heads.

I said, "I want to know everyone who was a part of those
films."

"You are in no position to dictate terms, Nathaniel."

"You're right. Give me the names anyway, Richie."

He stared at me like I was a ghetto child asking for a pony.
"Are you really that naive? What are you going to do? Chase
down each member of the film crew, case, and investors?"

"If I have to."

"You sound like a fool. It was her choice to make that film."

"No, I don't believe that."

Choices. Saint Augustine might be dry, but Shakespeare
wasn't. *There's small choice in rotten apples.* Whatever had driven
her into the basement, out onto the beach, and from her

window, hadn't been choice. Her death no more than her birth. There are wells too deep to climb up from, authority too established to escape, fears too familiar to overcome. Sutter sounded more the fool than me. "No one would choose that."

"You expose the fact that you did not know Susan as well as you think."

I didn't need to be reminded. "Maybe. But regardless, I'm going to find out who's behind this."

"Then you might begin by asking her father," he said, turning away.

Richie Sutter had finished with me, and I could feel him retracting his personality once more within his shell as he headed for the door. Three of the thugs filed out the door, one still left inside, waiting, guarding Richie until the end.

"Why?" I asked.

"Nathaniel, I told you I only had an investment in Semi-sweet Productions." He did smile then, far from a self-assured leer. The twisted mask of his face was anything but pleased, and an instant of intense communication bound us. "Lowell Hartford owns it."

***

I ran the tapes through twice more, needing to come to terms with who I was watching—a woman I had never known, and a woman I had become intimate with beyond anyone I'd ever met, but only in the grave. No matter how many times the events unfolded, I viewed only after-effects.

I took a shower, got dressed, went out and started my car. The rain had stopped, but the gutters rushed with water. Elms dripped soft *plish-plishes*. I drove for half an hour before I grew aware I was on my way to Montauk Point. The heater vehemently thrummed. Thoughts chewed up the two hours—fitting details. I grabbed the blanket out of the back seat and sat at the base of the lighthouse. Waves slapped rocks, and I could almost make myself see the flicker of a campfire down on the sand. *Would you like to make love to me?*

C'mon.

If only.

Life didn't move in circles, but it does, on occasion, repeat itself.

I enjoyed the loneliness.

My father sat in the sand beside me and showed me the face of the beast.

***

At nine-thirty the first beachcombers walked the dunes, and by ten a couple of rag-tag football teams of college kids were gathering on the field. Their girlfriends laughed as the guys practiced, catching over their shoulders and flopping other impressive moves.

I did a straight eighty MPH back home and drove directly to the library, understanding I'd missed something, and hadn't gone deep enough. It only took twenty minutes going through the microfiche to come across the article. I'd read it before. If I'd been a journalist instead of a novelist I would've been better suited for the dry facts.

Last pieces draw together as easily as first ones, but the picture, when completed, was like nothing I'd seen before. I kept re-reading the page, thinking of lost children, the ones left behind in my backyard and elsewhere, and however many more there might be.

I called Jordan.

***

At four o'clock she answered the door of the house on Dune Road. Gray shadows from the beaded water on the skylight speckled her forehead. Incredible that so many secrets had been kept hidden so long behind so much glass.

You couldn't see the window Susan had fallen from. I knew the patio furniture had been hauled off. For a few seconds, it seemed vastly important I find out if they had erased the last physical signs. That importance soon drifted away.

Jordan dressed in faded jeans, dark cashmere blouse, and white corduroy jacket, something she'd tossed on quickly so she could catch the earliest train back from the City. Her bountiful blond hair had been only partially sculpted. I'd caught her in the middle of her early afternoon routine. Worry lines crinkled the corners of her eyes, two smears of mascara gave her an Egyptian appearance. Since she wasn't smiling you couldn't see the dimples, and for some reason, that struck me hard.

"What is this about, Nathaniel? You wouldn't say anything over the phone."

I wanted to kiss and hold her, Christ, gather handfuls of her hair, and get back into bed for a week. The need to hold a beautiful, caring lady in my arms was greater now than when the feeling had driven me to Linda's. Jordan's voice was plaintive.

"Let me speak to your father."

"He's in his study, talking with Meachum."

She felt similar emotions; her hand reached up and stroked my cheek, fingertips grazing my beard stubble. She moved closer, nuzzling without touching, mouths only inches apart but neither of us covering the distance.

"What are you going to do?" she asked.

"That is the question."

Sarah Hartford stepped into the foyer, hands held up as if closing a purse not there. She was in immeasurably better shape than the last time I had seen her. A mildly sheepish smile creased her face. She had too much rouge to cover the pallor, but she was back in provisional control.

I knocked on the study door and let myself in. Lowell Hartford sat behind his desk in a broad-backed chair opposite Francis Meachum, who held several documents out to be signed. Hartford wasn't interested. He'd lost ten pounds, and most of them seemed drawn directly from his cheeks. He reminded me of my father, after insatiable cancer drained what was left of his life.

"You," he growled. It wasn't a particularly mean sound. "What are you doing in my home?"

There were a hundred responses to that question and most of them I didn't understand myself; a hundred more I would never be able to verbalize. *Because* wasn't a good enough reason, but it worked as well as any. It gathered sorrow and sex, desire, your pain and your past, and guilt, and bundled it all up into a neatly tied Pandora's box that would explode if you toyed with it too much.

Because would have been just fine, but I said, "I'm here to tell you why your daughter died."

The door shut behind me; Jordan and her mother had trailed me inside. Mrs. Hartford made a quiet noise—like a baby whimpering for its mother, a mother for its baby—but kept her face from cracking.

Meachum gaped. He still hadn't trimmed his nose hairs. "Eh?"

"You arrogant son of a bitch," Hartford said. "I'll have you locked up. Why are you disturbing my family?" He shoved aside a letter opener and paperweight, planting his fists on the desk between framed pictures of his children.

I said, "Trust."

Meachum stepped across the room as if to put his hands on me. "You'd better leave immediately, Follows. I'm going to the precinct and getting an order of protection against you." The muscles in my back bunched, and I felt the rage in a tight, warm feeling now in the pit of my stomach. It must've showed because he stopped in mid-motion. His toupee nearly slid onto his shoulder.

Lowell Hartford looked so much like my father it was throwing me off. Susan and Jordan smiled at me from the photos on the desk.

"There is a house in Dix Hills where pornographic videos are shot for your movie company Semi-sweet Productions."

"You're insane," Hartford said. The veins in his neck throbbed, black with blood. "I don't own any damn movie company."

"Yes, you do. I'm fairly sure you own the house, as well." His pointed eyebrows arched sharply, demonically rising. "The business is simply money generating money. Anonymously, except for the initial investment. That was the beauty of it. Nobody cared. It was, after all, only porn." He opened his mouth to berate or argue, but I cut him off. "Gabrielle Haney performed in those features as well as in the home-made underground films where she was beaten and degraded."

"Anthony Haney's daughter?"

Jordan pressed a hand to her mouth. Like Sutter, she had known Gabrielle most of her life. If only I'd thought to ask.

Lowell Hartford continued. "Just because he's a partner of mine in an international museum trade and ... and his daughter was allegedly wrapped up in pornography, doesn't mean I have anything to do with it."

"I know that."

His voice became even as a ruler. "Then what the hell are you saying?"

Jordan sat heavily in a chair. Her tone dripped. "Susan was involved, wasn't she, Nathaniel? In Richie's films?"

I wondered if Lowell Hartford had built ice castles with his daughters, if he'd ever taken the time away from his business affairs to make snow angels in the back yard. You could track your *ifs* for the rest of your life and willingly follow them wherever they might lead.

If only I'd read the articles more closely when checking up on Susan's family, I might have recalled the fact that he was usually out of the country with his partner, Anthony Haney.

I looked to Francis Meachum. "You're Anthony Haney's attorney also, aren't you?"

A small movement of his head could be considered a nod. I had to bite my tongue to keep from grinning. Without turning from Meachum I said, "Your children's trust fund was stolen, Mr. Hartford, and invested into a pornographic video production company in your name."

"Complete and utter nonsense!" Meachum shouted.

"That's redundant." I stood a foot from him. He took a step closer to the desk. I followed. The rage cooed. *So good. Do it.*

"What exactly are ..?"

A shade opened inside his eyes and I caught a glimpse of the real man moving around in there.

"How much? A quarter of a million? You took it, invested it, made the money back and returned the proper amount to where it belonged. I'm sure Semi-sweet Productions isn't the only venture." He rubbed his hands against his pants legs, then again, and again, getting them dry. He took another step towards the desk. "And you didn't do it because of the profit." Sweat dappled his jowls. He attempted to snarl at me but it came off more like a pig snorting. I tried not to think of what he looked like when raping Susan as a child, warping her self-worth, but the scenes flung themselves until I could barely see through them. The warmth in my gut turned cold.

His tongue slithered out and licked at his waxy lips.

"You should've dealt with someone who had more brains and better judgment. Frederic Malcomber was stupid. He told you I'd been asking questions at the club. The next day, when Jordan asked me to be here when her parents returned, you realized I wasn't going away. You called Malcomber and shadowed me. But as usual, One Freddy over-reached, taking matters into his hands. He tried to kill me in the fire and failed, and instead of solving problems he created more. The police were involved now, and John Brackman was nosing around as well—and you got scared someone would tie it to you. When Malcomber and I fought at The Bridge, you grew terrified of his over-reactions. Going crazy at the mention of Gabrielle's name was suspicious. When he killed Brackman you knew Malcomber had become too great a liability, so you killed him."

Jordan drew a breath. It was the first she'd heard that John was dead.

"I gave you the perfect opportunity to take him out, Meachum. With him gone, you thought there would be no connection left between you, the girls, and the videos."

He kept a straight face. "You have no evidence."

"I'm not a cop. I don't need any." That smell I'd mistakenly thought of as aftershave was still on him. "You stink of cherry blossoms and vanilla potpourri. You stink of that house."

"I'll bring you up on charges of libel!"

"You do that."

Brackman had either been smarter or crazier than I'd thought—either he'd had some notion Meachum was guilty or he'd suspected everybody and followed everybody.

"Brackman's pistol was unloaded when he got to Bluejay Drive. You found the bullets and loaded the gun, and although you must have wiped your prints from the butt and the trigger, I doubt you bothered to wipe the bullets themselves." His eyes bulged. "Common mistake," I said. I had no idea if the cops could dust bullets, but it was the the kind of thing I'd write in my books. "You might've thought of it if you'd ever read any mysteries."

Hartford delicately whispered, "You can't be serious."

"Oh my god," his wife said. "Francis? Is any of this the truth? Can any of it be true?"

Every nerve in my body was twice as sensitive as normal. I trembled slightly. "You were entrusted with the well-being of their families, but you abused their children, and twisted the girls so out of shape that masochism and suicide weren't choices, they became directions." My arms shook. "Child abuse. When one victim comes forward, others follow."

I hoped that what I was thinking was wrong. I didn't look behind me at Jordan. I prayed she'd escaped. Instead, I watched Lowell Hartford, kept my gaze pinned to his, and watched him staring at his one remaining daughter, and then saw his face crumble like cigarette ash.

Gentle, almost nurturing, her voice was of a victim who comes to care for the torturer, relying on abuse to give the abused an identity. *Who are you?* She said to Meachum, "You told me if I didn't say anything you wouldn't touch her."

Meachum took another step to the desk and made his move. He went for the paperweight, hefted it high, ready to bring it down on my skull.

The letter opener was already in my hand. I cut his throat ear to ear.

***

Eventually, someone made the phone call. Lieutenant Smithfield and two squad cars showed to clean up the endgame, but not until Hartford watched Meachum's blood pool at his shoes.

Smithfield listened attentively while cops questioned everybody and the EMTs stood in the doorway waiting to carry the corpse out. My head pounded, but this would be the last migraine for a while, I hoped. When I got up to leave, Jordan clung to her mother, sobbing—but her dimples flashed now and again. Lowell Hartford sat with the two women still left in his life and listened and talked and held them. Smithfield gave me one respectful nod.

***

Night fell fast. Lamp posts streamed with toilet paper. You could smell caramel-covered apples wafting through the neighborhood. Three Batmen ganged up on two Spidermen, wrestling each other over their bags. A dog barked behind a fence, furiously racing the length of its confines as the kids went by. Parents stood on sidewalks while children rushed driveways and rang doorbells. High-pitched giggling and shouts of "Trick or treat!" resounded across the block. Cars drove by slowly. Hedgerows were perfect ambush sites; eggs and shaving cream splattered the street. Baby Godzilla trudged up a front porch, hampered by stumpy dinosaur legs, nearly tumbling backwards into a bush if not for his Indian Chief brother there to steady him. A princess and a ballerina skipped by, watched closely by their free-spirited mother, who wasn't too adult to dress in Scarlett O'Hara regalia.

I thought of visiting Susan's grave. If this were my book, the Nathaniel Follows of the story would leave a bouquet of roses on freshly turned earth, find something honest but romanticized to say, and weave among the tombstones into the dawn. If it was a movie, the camera would back up high through the empty October branches, and you'd see Nathaniel kneel at the gravestone, and then stand after a lengthy pause to walk from her.

I started jogging. Ghosts ran beside me down the street, laughing with their hands thrust at me until I had nothing left to give. Finally, they turned away.

I kept going.